NO ANGEL HOTEL

NO ANGEL HOTEL

ANNE AYLOR

COLLINS · 8 Grafton Street, London, W1 · 1986

William Collins Sons & Co. Ltd.
London · Glasgow · Sydney · Auckland
Toronto · Johannesburg

First published 1986

BRITISH LIBRARY CATALOGUING IN PUBLICATION DATA

Aylor, Anne
No Angel Hotel.
I. Title
813'.54[F] PS3551.Y4/

ISBN 0–00–222942–1

Photoset in Linotron Plantin by Wyvern Typesetting
Made and printed in Great Britain by
William Collins Sons & Co. Ltd., Glasgow

For their help and encouragement, many thanks to

The Group, Rosalind Belben, Candyce Lange, Charles Walker,
Susan Hinchsliffe, Daphne Fontaine, Jean Caussin,
my parents, John and Alice Aylor, who taught me to love books
and as ever—*immer*—to P.

ACKNOWLEDGMENTS

The author is grateful for permission to quote from the following:

Post-War Russian Poetry edited by Daniel Weissbort, Copyright Daniel Weissbort 1974. 'Northern Elegies', 'The Sweetbriar Flowers' and 'Three Verses' by Anna Akhmatova translated by Richard McKane; 'Winter Night' and 'Parting' from *Doctor Zhivago* by Boris Pasternak translated by Richard McKane; 'Missing the Troop Train' by Yevgeny Vinokurov translated by Daniel Weissbort; untitled poem to I. Lavrentevaya by Natalya Gorbanyevskaya translated by Daniel Weissbort. Published by Penguin Books Ltd. Used by permission.

Anna Karenin by Leo Tolstoy translated by Rosemary Edmonds (Penguin Classics 1954), Copyright © Rosemary Edmonds 1954. Reprinted by permission of Penguin Books Ltd.

'The Love Song of J. Alfred Prufrock' and 'The Waste Land' from *Collected Poems 1909–1962* by T. S. Eliot. Reprinted by permission of Faber and Faber Ltd.

Wallflower by Deborah Turbeville. Reprinted by permission of Quartet Books Ltd. (Quoted on page 55 of this book.)

'Berck-Plage' from *Ariel* by Sylvia Plath, Copyright Ted Hughes 1965. Published by Faber and Faber Ltd. Used by permission.

'The Other' from *Winter Trees* by Sylvia Plath, Copyright Ted Hughes 1971. Published by Faber and Faber Ltd. Used by permission.

Excerpts from 'Spring in Fialta' by Vladimir Nabokov. Copyright 1947 by The Hearst Corporation. Reprinted from *Nabokov's Dozen* by permission of Doubleday & Company, Inc and William Heinemann Ltd.

Through the Looking Glass by Lewis Carroll. Reprinted by permission of Macmillan London Ltd. (Quoted on pages 83–84 of this book.)

'Emily Writes Such a Good Letter' and 'Beware the Man' (quoted on page 147 of this book) from *The Collected Poems of Stevie Smith*. Published by Allen Lane and Penguin Books Ltd. Reprinted by permission of James MacGibbon.

The Limit by Rosalind Belben. Reprinted by permission of Hutchinson Books Ltd.

'In the Orchard' from *Selected Poems* by Muriel Stuart. Reprinted by permission of Jonathan Cape Ltd.

Three Czech Poets (Penguin Modern European Poets 1971), Copyright © Ewald Osers and George Theiner 1970. 'Conception' and 'Those few years' by

Antonín Bartušek translated by George Theiner. Reprinted by permission of Penguin Books Ltd.
'One Trip Abroad' (quoted on page 122 of this book) and 'May Day' (quoted on page 127) from *The Bodley Head Scott Fitzgerald* by F. Scott Fitzgerald. Reprinted by permission of the Bodley Head, Ltd.
Under Milk Wood by Dylan Thomas. Published by J. M. Dent & Sons, Ltd. Used by permission.
'Night Time' by Victor Rowe. Used by permission.
'Before History' from *The Strange Museum* by Tom Paulin. Reprinted by permission of Faber and Faber Ltd.

Extracts from this book originally appeared in slightly different forms: 'The Hat' was read on BBC Radio 3, 1980; 'No Angel Hotel' was first published in *New Stories* 7, 1982.

for KIERAN

CONTENTS

I AUTUMN, 1966

Rustle of skirts, check plaids,
hazelwood frames of the mirrors
that are struck dumb by
Anna Karenina's beauty

Anna Akhmatova, 'Northern Elegies'

1

Two shoes fell
noisily on the floor.
Boris Pasternak, 'Winter Night'

And his mother said good night and we drank more sherry and he talked about Paris, how beautiful it is, the men fishing on the banks for gudgeon and the vines of the Seine that turn blood-red in the autumn and how small the *Mona Lisa* is.

He asked me if I'd done any travelling and I said I hadn't been out of the six counties, but that it was one of my dreams to go around the world. He smiled and poured me another glass of sherry. He wanted to know how old I was and what books I'd read, and said that he'd never seen hair like mine except in Italian paintings.

I pointed to the big canvas above the piano and said, 'That must be your da. You look just like him. Like Count Vronsky with dark hair!' And then his mouth went all twisted, and he told me he'd died when he was ten. He told me about the dream he'd had last night, about a coffin with a glass lid and black-and-gold sides, and the sound of banging as the horses pulled it down the road. His mother was walking in front of the cart in a big yellow hat, her arms full of lupins. He didn't know what the banging was, and when he looked into the casket he saw it was his father's head hitting the side of the coffin.

I started to cry. I felt like such a fool doing that in front of him, but it was the way he looked, like he was an orphan. He didn't want me to see him like that and he pretended to laugh. Said he didn't know why he was telling me that; it wasn't the sort of thing he'd ever tell anyone.

And then we drank more sherry and he took me upstairs. 'This used to be my room,' he said. It was so cold inside that we could see the spumes of our breath. 'Here are those tin soldiers I was telling you about.'

Near the bed was a chest covered with an army of them. I picked up a rusty drummer-boy and half the damn battalion fell over. 'Oh Jesus,' I said, trying to stand them up, 'I didn't mean to be so clumsy—'

He just laughed. 'Napoleon could have done with you at Waterloo.'

I was still trying to put them on their feet when he came over. 'Forget them,' he said. 'Aren't you cold?' And when I said yes, he put his arms around me. I felt his tongue in my ear and saw the strap of his mother's petticoat hanging below my elbow, but I didn't care. I heard myself telling him I'd been waiting for him every day at the avenue; I'd been waiting to see him again.

There was a fingernail moon. We danced—I can't think of any other word for it—all around the room, and his tongue was in my ear, my mouth. My knees kept giving way and then he'd pull me against him. I kept falling off my shoes.

I was shaking and he asked me what I was afraid of, and it must have been the drink because I said I wasn't afraid of anything.

'Not even the dark?' he whispered.

'Not even the dark.' And on the floor, before the lights went out, I saw that beautiful dress and my shoes upside down on the carpet. It was all that sherry. I was reckless with the sherry.

I was reckless with him. He touched me where I had never been touched before and I let him. I wanted him. I wanted him more than anything.

I closed my eyes; those toy soldiers saw everything.

2

You and I met in an improbable year, . . .
Without lamps the Neva was black as pitch.
Anna Akhmatova, 'The Sweetbriar Flowers'

A half-mile from Pellipar House was an avenue of trees. Viewed from the front it was two trunks with many branches, from the side a long windbreak of evenly-planted birches. They stood naked except for a fresh coat of lime which dressed them halfway up their trunks.

At the mouth of the avenue was a large puddle which formed there after heavy rain. A young woman stood facing it. She wore a black cardigan and a dark skirt that was too long. Her red hair was shoulder-length, frizzy; her feet were covered in leaves. One of her socks bagged on her leg leaving her calf exposed. She looked hesitant, off-balance as she leaned over the water to see her reflection.

Ophelia, he thought and called out, 'What are you doing here?'

Startled, she jumped back from the edge of the water. 'Are you from the house?' she said.

'Yes.'

'You're not going to report me are ye?'

'Report you?' He laughed. 'Whom shall I report you to?' He liked the way her thin skirt had wrapped itself around and between her legs, clinging to her stockings.

'I know I'm trespassing, but it's so beautiful here.' She moved towards a bicycle lying in the leaves. 'There's never anyone about. Not usually.' She struggled to pick up the bicycle and in her haste, dropped it. The handlebars twisted up like horns.

'Here, let me help you.' He lifted the heavy, old bicycle and steadied it. 'There. Now the beast's under control.'

'That's kind of you, sir, really kind.' She smiled and brushed the hair away from her face. 'What are you doing at the avenue? Are you new at the house?' and when he started to laugh, she knew. Those high cheekbones, that patrician face, the way he held himself: like a count, or a soldier. Sweet Jesus, she thought. 'Then you must be Ivan,' she said. 'Are you Ivan?'

'The prodigal son himself. And what's your name then?'

'It's Luz. L-U-Z Bonner.'

'Luz? That's Spanish. A strange name for a Protestant around here.'

'Oh I'm a descendant of one of the sailors from the Armada.'

That's too confident for you, he thought, it came out too fast. He smiled. 'And what's the rose of Castille doing on my land then? Poaching?'

'Oh no.' She blushed and shook her head. 'Nothing like that. I just came for a wee ride on my bike.'

'I'll tell you a secret, Miss Bonner. When I was a boy, this was my favourite place. I sailed boats here with my father. He said the wee folk—' He paused here because 'the wee folk' was something she would have said. He sensed she'd like to hear him say it, because it would make the difference between them less great. 'My father said the wee folk danced here, that they stomped out this hollow with their boots. We had some great sea battles here. We had a flotilla we manned with tin soldiers. In our naval battles there were a lot of casualties on both sides. I used to worry about the ones that had fallen overboard, but my father assured me that this was an enchanted place. He said the faeries would take grand care of the ones that had drowned.'

He knelt and picked up a stone and threw it into the water. 'As a child I always found that thought rather reassuring. Well Miss Bonner, I've done my duty. Now that I know you're not poaching, I can go home.' He winked. She would remember that wink for years.

He started to walk away. He was whistling, the case banging against his leg. She started to run after him pushing the bicycle, the heels of her shoes catching in the mud.

She wheeled the bicycle between them. 'I thought . . . I thought that I might go this way home for a change. Do ye want to balance your bag up here on the seat?'

He shook his head. 'Thanks, but it's not that far now to the house.'

'I live in the town,' she blurted out. 'Me da runs the grocery store. Bonner's Grocery.'

'Oh,' he said smiling, 'I'd never have guessed.'

They walked slowly down the row of trees in silence and then she suddenly said, 'I hope you're not angry with me for trespassing.'

'Should I be?'

'You seemed angry when you saw me standing there.'

'I wasn't. Just surprised to find anyone at the avenue. How did you know my name?'

'Oh everyone in the town knows it.'

'So she still goes to the Holy Romans and pays them to say Mass for the return of my soul!' He laughed. 'My mother always did think that Catholics were better equipped to pray for the damned than we were.'

'You know about that?' she said. 'How'd you know about that?'

'As you're no doubt aware, Miss Bonner, my mother has had the reputation of doing strange things for years.' He looked straight ahead, not wanting her to see the look of disgust on his face.

'So what if she is different?' she said. 'At least she's not afraid to do what she feels. She's not a hypocrite. She keeps to herself and minds her own business. Not like the rest of them in Dungiven.'

He didn't answer and she was suddenly afraid of his silence, afraid of the coldness that had come into his voice when he spoke about his mother. It was as numbing to her as the handlebars in her ungloved hands.

They were at the end of the avenue when she blurted out, 'Because you told me a secret, I'll tell you one. I wasn't telling the whole truth when I said I'd just come for a ride. I like to come here because it reminds me of Russia. I know that sounds mad, but it does. Those huge trees like that in the middle of a field. It's not like that anywhere else around here.'

He smiled and she smiled, he thought, a doll's smile. A cheap carnival-doll's smile because it was just a little crooked and poorly painted.

3

And it seems something happened there
that it's better not to look into, we will go away.
Anna Akhmatova, 'Northern Elegies'

Sarah sat in the oak-back chair facing the lawn and neat, clipped hedges. Ice-white hair fell past her shoulders. She was staring at the bare branches of the rose trees outside the window.

Approaching her sitting in her throne like that, so rigid and imperious, she looked every inch the faded aristocrat she was, that and something else he could not quite remember.

'Here's a wee cup of tay in your hand, mother,' he said. The colloquial inflection of his voice shocked him because it was not his own; it was the girl's. He'd carried their meeting into the dampness of the house with him.

His mother looked at him in surprise. 'Why are you talking like that, Ivan?' she said, taking the cup and saucer from him. 'I haven't heard you use that accent for years.'

'I was talking to some girl from the village.'

'I thought it rather odd,' she said. 'Since you were ten you've always pretended you were English.'

She held out her hand. 'Come here and give your mother another kiss. Why didn't you let me know you were coming? If you'd warned me I could have aired the rooms, bought some decent port. Made things nice again.'

Things were never nice here, he thought, but he didn't say that. 'I didn't tell you, mother, because I knew you'd go to too much trouble.'

'Why didn't you come to see me sooner?' she teased him.

'You know how much it means to an old woman. You wouldn't have come home now if I hadn't told you that hectare was being auctioned. Why don't you think seriously of coming back to Northern Ireland to live?'

'My work is my life, mother.'

'You could work here. We could manage the estate together; we wouldn't have to hire outsiders to manage our affairs.'

'Why don't we sell Pellipar? Lately it's been more trouble to you than it's worth.'

'Don't be absurd, Ivan. It's just that the house is too much for me to cope with alone.'

'Why don't you have a domestic live in?'

'Because they gossip and break things. What would there be for them to do? I live in three rooms. Besides, at my age I can't stand to have strangers in the house. I don't want anyone in the house now except you.'

He walked to the piano at the far side of the room. A portrait of his father was centred above it in an ornate, Italian frame. He wiped some dust from the glass. 'As you loved him so much,' she said, 'it must be a comfort to know that you look just like he did. Even your smile. You wouldn't think you could inherit a smile, would you?'

He seated himself at the piano. The ivory keys had crazed and darkened; they were the colour of her teeth.

'That's a pretty mazurka,' she said. 'Do continue. It's been such a long time since there was music in this house.' She watched him play, glancing from the music to the canvas and back again. 'Your father had a nice smile really. Like a bloody Tartar.'

She sighed and leaned back into her chair. 'I've always hated this room. Willie died in here. The poor, little thing died in my arms. Maybe it was better he never grew up. He never had to suffer like some of us. Do you remember how we used to visit his grave? Every Sunday we'd take your brother a bouquet of flowers from the garden.'

'Do you ever go now?'

'No!' she snapped. 'I've not gone since your father drowned. I couldn't face that mocking headstone, Gone But Not Forgotten.' She twisted her loose hair into a rope. 'God, I don't know how I could have been so maudlin. His mistress would have chosen something more eloquent, don't you think? Helen Doran would have built a mausoleum to their deathless love.'

'Mother—'

'Why didn't she die with him? But Helen wouldn't drown. She always was the strong one. James was the romantic and the coward.' She pressed her shoulders against the high-backed chair. 'No,' she said, 'allow me to correct myself. Your father was just a coward.'

Her son continued to play, never once breaking rhythm. 'I know you've never said one word against him, but I've never forgiven him. I'll never forgive him for drowning.'

'Why don't you play something, mother? Something you used to play.' He pulled the piano bench out for her.

'You're not listening to a word I say,' she said, 'so I might as well.'

As she walked towards him, she stroked her hair. With it long like that, white and uneven, he knew now what it was that she had reminded him of sitting in her chair: the cold, blue illustration of the Ice Queen in his old book of faery-tales.

'You choose something.' He handed her a stack of yellowed sheet music.

'Thank you,' she said. 'And while we're still on serious subjects, Ivan, why haven't you married? They say all men should marry. You're almost thirty-five. You're not getting any younger.'

'Allow me to correct you. I believe Disraeli said, "Every woman should marry—and no man." '

'But Disraeli was a bachelor. You'd expect a bachelor to say that. He didn't have an estate to think about. He didn't have land to pass on.' She put some music on the stand and flattened the binding with her fingers. 'You know it's not just that. I want to see my grandchildren before I die. I'm not going to live forever. Half of us are dead already.'

He ignored her and picked up the photograph album from the side-table. Inside the front cover was a picture of his father. He was standing in front of the garden sundial; it was powdered with snow.

'What are you looking at?' she said.

'Father's last picture.'

'I should have guessed.' She stood up and held the unmounted photograph next to her son's face. 'You're almost the same age now as he was then. The same chin, eyes, that bloody smile.' The picture sailed across the room.

'Don't pick it up,' she said. 'You really are two of a kind. Underneath your English veneer you despise me just as much as he did.' She rubbed her arms and turned away. 'Shall we have a fire?' she said. 'It's absolutely perishing in here.'

Kneeling on the hearth he arranged the logs. She's cold, he thought, so bloody cold. I'll build a fire, a roaring winter's fire, and watch the Ice Queen slowly melt into her shiny, satin shoes.

In the silence of the sitting-room she picked up her embroidery hoop. 'Why don't you ever come to see me, Ivan? It's more than four years since your last visit.'

'You know I'm abroad a great deal.'

'You could have made time to see me if you'd wanted to. By the way, did you find what you were looking for in your father's room? You were looking for his diary, weren't you?'

He looked up from the hearth. 'How did you know about that?'

'I may be old, but I'm not senile. Why don't you just ask me for it? I can save you so much time.'

'You know why. You refused to give it to Helen when she came here for it.'

Her face leaned closer to the linen. Her fingers worked quickly, jerking the thread. 'So she sent you for it. Her errand boy, her lackey. So you inherited that from James too. Don't you know when I saw you creeping through his door, I realized why you were here? You didn't come to see me or to get a better price for that land. You came to steal his diary. For her. For Helen Doran. Aren't you the loyal son? Well, aren't you? You'd never have known that diary existed if she'd kept her bloody mouth shut like she was paid to! You shouldn't rake up the past. Are you listening to me, Ivan? You'll only burn your fingers.'

He turned his back to her, squatted at the hearth again. He stared into the fire, then quickly passed his fingers once, twice, three times through the flames.

The next afternoon Elkie left the grocery shop early and went home. She carefully applied her mother's lipstick. She felt more sophisticated with a red mouth. She hated the naked shape of her lips. Painting them made her look and feel older; colour falsified their childish Cupid's bow.

She took the old bicycle out of the shed and rode along the lane until she passed the caretaker's dilapidated cottage at the back entrance to Pellipar. She followed the narrow, muddy path until she came to the avenue of trees. She laid the bicycle in the leaves and waited for him to come. She was certain that he'd be there, but when he wasn't, she waited.

She sat at the puddle, writing in a notebook to pass the time: Ethel Louise Bonner mutated to Elkie Bonner and then to Luz: Luz, Luz, Luz scrawled authoritatively across the page. She'd read it in a romance magazine once and had been fascinated by its poetic meaning. The story had said it meant light; it was the Spanish word for 'light of the snows'.

With the certainty of a child she knew he would be there, and when he wasn't, she waited with her new name. She waited for three hours. It began to rain.

He spent the afternoon reading. He could hear his mother in the kitchen banging pots and pans. She shouted, 'You don't know how difficult it is to make a perfect béchamel sauce. You have no idea.'

He called back, 'How often do you make béchamel sauce?'

'When you come.'

'When you come,' he muttered. He slammed the book shut and threw it on the couch. 'I really wish you wouldn't go to so much trouble—'

'Don't you know that nothing is too much trouble for a mother? Talk to me,' she shouted, 'you'll soon be rid of me. I could tell by the size of your case you wouldn't be staying long. And while I'm thinking of it, I want to show you something. As you're home so infrequently, there's something we need to settle.'

The smell in her room was the same, that mournful smell of lavender and violets. Everything was covered in a skin of dust. As his mother unlocked the cedar wardrobe, he glanced up; the ceiling light was full of dead insects.

Sarah took out a skein of twisted silk; it unfolded into a gas-blue gown with mushroom pleats. 'My father bought me this dress,' she said, stroking it. 'It's a Fortuny. They call it the "Delphos" dress because it looked like the drapery on a statue at Delphi. I was married in it. Blue! Can you imagine? I refused to wear white. I did it to shock the congregation. They were shocked enough as it was, me being pregnant with Willie.'

She laughed and pressed the dress against her shoulders. 'Now when I die, Ivan, this is the dress I want to be buried in.'

'Mother, really—'

'Don't look at me like that. We have to discuss these things. Of all the things I own, this means the most to me. I've become a practical woman in my old age. I've lived alone too long.'

She opened the jewellery case on top of the vanity and dangled an opal necklace from her fingers. 'And I want to wear this. This was a gift from your father before we were married, before everything began to go wrong. We weren't happy except then. I want to take some memory of happiness with me. I've had so little of it.'

He forced himself to look at his mother, at her pale, powdered face, the dangerous redness of her mouth.

'You think I'm mad, don't you? I can tell by the way you're looking at me. Just like an Englishman, trying so hard to hide it! Well, I was mad in my youth. In our set at Oxford we all were. We surrendered everything to passion. We were still aping the Fitzgeralds when the Jazz Age was dead. Our set was elegant and daring. We used to gad about a lot in cars. I had lots of lovers before your father. Did you know that? Well I did. More than I could count, but James was the only one that I loved. I wasn't really mad. The truth is that I loved him. I loved him too much; that was my crime. And look at me now. I'm an old recluse who has nothing but her memories. You wouldn't think to look at me now that I was beautiful once. That I was whole.'

She turned towards the mirror, a look of revulsion on her face. She stretched the wrinkled skin on her brow, the tips of her fingers dusted with face powder. Seeing them, she screamed. 'The sauce!'

As he followed her downstairs he heard a crash in the kitchen; when he came into the room a pan was on the floor. Behind the stove béchamel sauce dribbled down the wall.

'Why are you looking at me like that?' she said. 'It curdled. You must know a well-mannered béchamel sauce isn't supposed to behave that way.'

4

A roaring in his ears since morning.
Is he conscious or dreaming?
And why does the thought of the sea
creep unceasingly into his mind?
Boris Pasternak, 'Parting'

Ivan passed the church; he walked until he reached the far side of the graveyard. At the foot of his father's plot was a ceramic wreath mounted on a tripod, at its head the polished granite slab with the inscription his mother so hated.

He picked up a vase that had fallen over, the paper flowers in it just beginning to melt. Helen's, he thought, and threw them out. She had been here last month.

Ivan knelt and cleared the wet leaves away with his hands. He didn't bother with the smaller, adjacent plot. He'd never known his brother William; he'd died of typhus a few months before he was born.

'Afternoon, sir. Back home for a wee visit?' He looked up to see Gandy Scott. Gandy wasn't his real name; that was what everyone called him. That long neck like a gander's, a gander's neck to be able to see out of the grave.

'How are you keeping, Mr Scott?'

'I'm keepin' fine. It's hard to keep up with the work but. There's a lot of people dyin'. I suppose we all have to go sometime. You stayin' long?'

'Just a few days.'

'I heard you got a good price for that piece of land you was sellin'.'

'News travels fast.'

'Well, there's not much to talk about around here. And how's your mother keepin'?'

'She's fine. Still complaining she never sees me.'

'Aye, surely. Well she's glad she hasn't seen me. Still you know women, sir. They're like that. When you're there, they're complainin' so's if it's not one thing, it's another. Well, I'd better get back to me work. All the best t'ya see ye again.' He touched his cap and then walked in the direction of the shed.

He was glad when Gandy Scott was gone; to be alone again, not to have to make small talk. And like everyone else in the town, he felt uneasy in his presence. They said Gandy Scott sized up the living for the grave like he did with the dead.

Ivan arranged the cut flowers in the vase and set it near the headstone. He stood at the foot of the grave, cap in hand. Gone But Not Forgotten. Gone, but not forgotten. *'Over my dead body,' Sarah told me. 'I'll never give you a divorce so you can marry her. I've already lost Willie. I won't lose you.'* The last entry in his father's diary; he had found it that morning.

He had never known it existed, not until Helen had asked him to find it. In exchange, he had forced her to make a promise. He would keep the diary and only hand it over to her when he wanted to know the truth about his father. 'You're mad,' she'd said. 'Better to let sleeping dogs lie.'

But he was the only one who could get her the diary; she was the only one who could tell him the truth about that night. She had been with James rowing, rowing on the River Roe, the night that he had drowned.

Ivan tightened his muffler and tucked it into his coat. He turned to go back to the house. It was a good twenty-minutes' walk. He had walked a lot since he'd been home. It'd given him time to be alone, to think. He'd be gone soon anyway. There was just tonight to get through and after dinner, when he'd run out of things to argue with her about, he could always get drunk.

As he neared the avenue he thought of the strange girl with red hair, that doll's smile. If he was honest, she was the one he wanted to get drunk. He started up the steep hill that led to the row of birches and imagined her flying past him on her ancient bicycle, her Burne-Jones hair blown backwards.

At the top of the rise he saw her. She was sitting at the mouth of the avenue by the vlei, her legs folded beneath her. 'Oh it's you!' she said as he approached her. She tried to hide the book she was reading beneath her skirt.

'What don't you want me to see?'

Sheepishly, she handed him the battered paperback. 'It's just a wee book I'm reading.'

'That's the first time I've heard *Anna Karenina* called wee.'

'I guess it's not really wee.'

He opened the book and read the first sentence aloud. ' "All happy families are alike but an unhappy family is unhappy after its own fashion." ' He smiled. 'I'd say Count Tolstoy had that right. And what are you doing sitting on the ground in this weather?'

'Just reading. I like reading here.'

'But you're soaking wet.'

'I don't mind the damp,' she said. 'I quite like the damp.'

'Want up?' She nodded; he reached down. It amused him that once she'd found her balance she had kept his hand longer than she'd needed to.

He wheeled around and pointed at her bicycle. 'Aha! I recognize those markings! That beast has wandered onto my property again. I shall have to take it into custody for trespassing. Don't laugh, Miss Bonner, this is a dangerous business.'

He circled the bicycle cautiously, then jumped away. 'Did you see that?' he said. 'Did you see that? It tried to gore me! This isn't going to be as simple as I'd planned. I'm going to need help to herd this animal back to the house. What I really need is someone who knows its obstreperous character better than I do—'

They sat at the dining-room table which seated twelve. His mother cut the Battenburg cake and put the largest slice on the girl's plate. 'I hope that's enough for you, dear,' she said. 'I apologize if I appear to be staring. I just can't get over how lovely you look.'

She had the Fortuny on; his mother had insisted that she wear it to dinner. It was the only thing in her wardrobe that was fashionable enough for a young girl to wear.

'. . . that dress is a classic. Father bought it for me in Paris. It cost twelve pounds in the 'thirties. Twelve pounds was a lot of money in those days. But it was worth it. The style is ageless and it does suit you terribly, I must say. It really shows off a girl's figure. Ivan, don't you think she looks just captivating in that dress? You see? He agrees with me.'

Elkie looked across the table at him and blushed. She couldn't stop her cup rattling when she put it back on its saucer.

'Did you know that Ivan's not married? He travels a great deal in his work. It's difficult to meet people if you're constantly travelling. I've been trying to persuade him to marry, but he never listens to a word I say.'

'Can I help you clear away the plates, mother? Excuse us, Luz, won't you? We won't be long.' She watched them as they walked stiffly towards the lit rectangle at the far end of the room, and then closed the door.

She stood up; she started to dance. She felt like she was in a dream. She slapped her knees, ran her hands over her breasts, her thighs, fingered the tiny, swirled-glass beads sewn on the sides of the dress. She'd have to remember to keep her left arm hidden; the skin on her forearm was red where she'd pinched it all through dinner.

'Mother, do behave yourself,' he whispered in the corridor. 'Don't frighten her.'

'Frighten her?' Sarah looked at him in surprise. 'How could I frighten her?'

'All that rubbish about marriage for a start. You shouldn't say leading things like that in front of her; she's very impressionable. She could hardly hold her cup. And for God's sake, don't bore her with any more family history.'

'I'm only trying to amuse her. You're not saying much. She's hardly said a word. Someone has to talk.'

'I'll help out with the conversation if you promise not to finish your saga.'

'Which saga's that? According to you I have so many.'

'The one about grandfather supervising the building of the *Titanic*.'

'She said she was interested in ships.'

'She'd say she was interested in Timbuktu just to please you. You're wicked,' he said taking her arm, 'letting her wear that bewitching gown to dinner.'

'Aren't I?' She smiled. 'Well, what about showing her the eggs then? She wouldn't be bored with that.'

'All right.'

'What's her name again?'

'She calls herself Luz.'

'Luz. That *is* a strange name. I must practise it. Luz, Luz—

'Luz,' she said, throwing open the door.

The sound of silverware clattering to the floor. The girl picked up the fork, put it next to her plate. 'I was only looking at the hallmark. I wasn't trying . . . I hope ye don't think—'

'Don't be ridiculous, my dear girl. I'm certain the silver's all there. Fortuny gowns reveal everything. Now before I take myself off to bed, there's something I'd like to show you.'

She led her to the afrormosia cabinet in the sitting-room. 'This is where I keep my eggs. I've been collecting them for more years than I'd care to count.' She turned the key in the glass door's lock. 'Ivan's under strict orders to buy me unusual eggs whenever he's abroad. Last month he sent me this crystal one from Paris. Here, you can look at it if you like.'

'Oh isn't it a brilliant, wee egg!' She cupped it carefully in her hands as if it were some live thing, a bird, a chick about to hatch.

'I started blowing eggs when Ivan was small. The eggs I decorated myself are in addition to the ones we've purchased over the years. The big one in the middle is a papier-mâché egg from Kashmir, those wooden ones in the basket are from Poland. That brightly-coloured one at the back is from what was once known as St Petersburg.'

'St Petersburg? Oh can I see that one, please?'

'Of course. I'll hand it out to you.'

'It's beautiful! It's perfect. Just perfect.'

'It's a blown egg. I think it's useful to know how to blow an egg. It's one thing in this transient life you can lock up and keep forever.'

He walked over to the cabinet and whispered, 'Why don't you go to bed, mother? It's after midnight. The port's made you quite drunk.' He leaned over Elkie's chair. 'A refill?'

'Sherry'd be brilliant.' She smiled that carnival-doll smile again and asked, 'What's Paris like? I've always dreamt of going to Paris.'

He filled her glass, then his own. 'Paris, where shall I start? It's an old city full of trees and wide boulevards. Because it's so old, nothing is simple there. It's old and young at the same time. And beautiful. Like you.' And, he thought, it's the scotch that's made you say that.

But if he was honest with himself, it wasn't just that. It was that and her innocence, her Renaissance hair. Her open Gonzaga mouth smiling up at him.

5

If he could have heard the conversation between
her parents that evening, if he could have put
himself in her family's place . . . he would
have been greatly astonished and not believed it.

Leo Tolstoy, *Anna Karenina*

Through the drawn curtains a splinter of light embedded itself into the floor. He focused on it for a moment not knowing where he was, not until he turned over and saw her lying on the bed. He groaned. He did such foolish things when he was drunk, the things he had done or said, only half-remembered.

Why did I bring her back to the house, he thought, why? But he knew why; it was because he was vulnerable here. At home he had to face those things that anywhere else he could always push to one side: his father's grave, his mother's anger, the death he did not, as a boy, believe was death. In Frankfurt they'd buried their dead with bells on their fingers to prevent premature inhumation.

He looked at her, her hair spread out on the pillow, and remembered that he'd told her about that dream, the nightmare about his father. He'd told her it was his father's head banging against the side of the coffin, but it was not his head. It was his fists, his fists hammering against the *Risorgimento* sides, the glass. He'd told her he'd had that dream the night before, but he had lied about that. He'd had that dream for years, for years he'd woken up screaming in the night.

For a week after his father's funeral he refused to speak. He had found them that day in the greenhouse, Helen Doran and his father. They were naked, wrapped in each other's arms, clutching each other's necks as though they were drowning.

6

And indeed there will be time
To wonder, 'Do I dare?' and, 'Do I dare?'
T. S. Eliot, 'The Love Song of J. Alfred Prufrock'

'You have no business going off like this. No business, d'ye hear? For crissakes, you don't even know the man.' Her father paced the length of the parlour. Only the red hurricane lamp in the corner was lit. It cast long shadows across the polished floor.

'If you don't give me your blessing to go away, daddy, I'll go without it. I'm not a minor any more.'

'D'ye hear that, Marion? Turned twenty-one not two months ago and thinks that gives her the liberty to turn against her own father.'

'I'm not turning against you and ye know it. It's my life.'

'It may be your life, but it's my reputation that'll suffer for it. What will I say to them down at the shop when they're asking me all sly-like where my wee daughter's gone to? "Oh don't you know," I'll be saying to them, "our Elkie's run off to London with the loon's prodigal son!" '

'Tell them what ye like. It's none of their business anyhow.'

'Well missie, it's our business.' He banged his fist on the table; the budgerigars in the corner began to sing. He wheeled around to accuse his wife. 'Didn't I tell you to stop her reading that book? Didn't I? It's that damn Russki book she carts around all the time that's put these ideas about sex into her head.'

'For God's sake, daddy, what would you know about books? You've never read a bloody book in your life.'

'D'ye hear what she said? D'ye hear what she said? Don't just stand there gawking at those damn birds, Marion! For cris-sakes, say something!'

'The wee budgies are out of cuttlebone,' she said although they were not out of it at all.

'Christbetojesus! My only daughter's talking about running away with a man and you, and all you can talk about is cuttlebone! Has the whole world gone mad? Has everyone in this house gone stark, raving mad?'

They watched his shadow grow shorter as he marched across the room. The family portrait slid to the left when he slammed the door. Marion let her hand drop from the cage. She walked slowly over to the picture and straightened it. She'd told her husband to talk things over calmly with Elkie, that to oppose her leaving openly would only increase her determination to go.

'You'll have to forgive your da his ranting and raving. He's obviously forgotten what it feels like to be in love.' She turned around and smiled wanly at her daughter. 'You think you love him, don't you? Jesus Christ, I don't know why I'm asking you that. It's all over your wee face,' and she felt like crying then, but there would be enough time for that after her daughter was gone.

She walked to the window and slid her hands into the pockets of her dressing gown. 'You're right when you say we can't prevent your leaving, but you can't blame us for wanting to stop you doing something we feel to be wrong. But you've got a conscience, Elkie. You're the one that's going to have to sleep with it.'

She leant against the window, put her head against the glass. 'Before you go pack, I'd like you to answer me just one question. Elkie, when I was young I loved your da so much I would have died for him. Do you love like that?'

The old suitcase lay open on the bed. Dresses, slips, books lay in heaps on the floor. Elkie folded a pink sweater and put it on top of the packed clothes. She made a funny face in the mirror glued to the lid. She was ashamed of meeting him at the house with this old case. One of the catches didn't close properly; the brown sides were dented and scratched. There'd been no time to buy a new one. He hadn't given her time.

Said he was leaving and would she come with him, just like that. 'We'll have to run away together,' he said, 'now that you're a fallen woman. Be at the door tomorrow night, quarter to seven, sharp.'

He'd been drunk when he said it. He didn't plan to say it, his face had told her that, but before he could compose himself enough to take it back, she had said, 'Yes!' Without stopping to take a breath.

Elkie ran over to the dressmaker's dummy and hugged it, cradling its unresponsive weight in her arms. The way he had touched her, the way she had stumbled around the room, his tongue deep in her mouth. That beautiful dress like water; it had rippled when she'd worn it. And when he had slipped it off her, a still, cool pool on the bedroom floor. She had left him with a sea inside her, blue, blue, like the colour of that dress.

Remembering, she cried and squeezed the dummy tighter. 'Of course I'll run away with you, Count Vronsky! Haven't I been waiting for you for the whole of me life? Sure, I'd follow you to Moscow! To the Dardanelles and St Petersburg—'

'Elkie Bonner!' Her mother's anxious voice from the stairs. 'Who are ye talking to?'

'Meself.'

'You're too young to be talking to yourself. Now you be sure to take a pair of scissors with ye. Ye'll always be needing scissors.' Her mother was standing in the doorway. 'I just phoned your gran to tell her you were going to London to do a secretarial course, and she said she'd buy you that angora sweater you were admiring as a going-away present.'

'Did she? Did she really?'

'Now remember about that course and don't slip up when you write to her. She said it'd go with that kick-pleat skirt she gave you for your birthday. Look sweetheart, you should fold them like this.' Her mother lifted out the tangled clothes. 'You can get more in if you fold them flat.'

She shook the clothes out and made a space for folding on the bed. 'Your gran said to tell you as you're leaving so soon, she'd post the sweater on to ye.'

'That's brilliant!' She smiled at her mother, then jerked her arm. 'How's me da? Is he still raging?'

'He's still raging all right, but he'll get over it. He'll just have to. Times have changed since we were courting. Mind ye, he seems a decent enough fella from what you've told me. He'll not see you short of a bob or two. All the same, Elkie, for your own sake, I do wish you were married.'

She continued, more slowly now, folding the clothes. She was thinking of her honeymoon, the hotel where they had first shared a bed, their bodies.

The Angel Hotel. They had a small room with a window overlooking the alleyway. There were the essentials: a bed, a wardrobe, a sink. No mirror or small bars of paper-wrapped soap. She went out the next morning while he was still asleep and bought the mirror and epoxy glue, and pressed it to the suitcase's sateen lid. She wanted to see if she looked any different, how brides looked. In between her legs was wet and there were drops of it on the linoleum floor in the loo. He was lying in bed with a silly smile on his face, and she knew how much she loved him and how happy she was, and to show him she undressed again and slipped into bed, and touched his bare back with the tips of her fingers.

She wanted to tell her daughter that, to tell her those things, but she could not. 'Well,' she said, 'that's your clothes all done. A word of advice. Don't you be taking up smoking in London. You never know what's in cigarettes these days. Now you must promise me you'll write. You know how much your da dotes on ye. I'll put a writing pad and some stamped envelopes in the bottom so's you won't forget. Just a letter every week or so to let us know how you're getting on.'

Before she closed the case she traced a finger once around the looking glass. 'You know, Elkie, your da and I took this case with us on our honeymoon. Our wee room didn't have a mirror so I bought this, and glued it in.'

There was silence in the room now though they were both so full of words. Then her mother's voice again, hesitant, scratchy as though she'd been asleep a hundred years and had woken up again, and was trying with great difficulty to talk. 'I know we've never talked about it, Elkie, but I'm sure ye know there are precautions. I just hope to God ye have the sense to take precautions.'

7

'My nerves are bad to-night. Yes, bad. Stay with me.
'Speak to me. Why do you never speak. Speak.
T. S. Eliot, 'The Waste Land'

The flat was in a row of terraced houses clinging to a steep hill. Elkie checked the house number against that of the advertisement's; they matched. She hid her suitcase behind the garden wall, marched up the peeling plaster steps and pressed her finger, hard, on the ceramic nipple of the bell.

A heavy woman, heavy with sleep, answered the door. She looked shapeless in the purple kimono she wore, a puce tie-belt delineating a waist that was not there. 'What do you want?' she said.

'I've come about the room, the one advertised in the *Evening Standard*.'

The fat woman folded her arms. 'So you've come about the room have you? I'll have you know you got me out of bed. I have a lie-in on a Saturday. Come back when the pigeons are up.' She started to slam the door.

'Wait,' the girl said, blocking its path. She was thinking of the night she'd just spent in Victoria Coach Station, those uncomfortable two weeks with Helen Doran. 'I've got an appointment later. If you want to show me that room, I've got the time to see it now.'

The woman sighed in exasperation. 'You're a persistent little Paddy, aren't you? You can count your lucky stars it wasn't Mr Ducker who answered the bell. He would have shown you the door soon enough.' The landlady looked her sharply up and down. 'Oh . . . all right. Since you've already woken me up.'

She shuffled across the hall in her mules and disappeared into a room at the back. She returned still wearing the mules, but dressed in a shift patterned with red pagodas. She jingled a ring of keys. 'What's your name then?'

'Elkie Bonner.'

'Well, Miss Bonner, Mr Ducker and I are choosy who we take on as our tenants. We don't take every Tom, Dick and Harry that comes knocking at our door—'

'I don't blame ye,' she interrupted. 'You get a lot of riffraff in London.'

'We only rent to respectable girls.' Mrs Ducker addressed her remark to Elkie's sensible shoes. 'I'll warn you right now, you're the sixth we've shown the room to.'

Stilettos, flip-flops, ballerina pumps? On the way upstairs Elkie tried to picture what damning footwear the others had worn. The landlady was gasping. 'Up one . . . up one more flight. It's at the top of the house.' Mrs Ducker was still panting when she unlocked a door on the third-floor landing.

It was a large room, a large room made small with furniture. Leaf-table, wardrobe, two armchairs, sideboard, coffee-table, bed: all abnormally large and heavy, solid enough to withstand another war.

The kitchen had its own door. Above the stove was a sagging shelf lined with empty jars, a clay water jug, a lidless teapot. 'Now that you've seen it, what do you think?'

'It's grand,' Elkie said, running her hand over the monolithic bed, 'it's a grand, wee room.'

'Like I was saying before, Mr Ducker and I only rent to respectable girls. The one next door's an audio typist, the three on the second floor are secretaries, then there are some Frenchies learning to speak the language on the first. Well,' she said, 'do you want it or not?'

'I'll take it.'

'Good. I'll tell you a few things about the place. Light, electricity, gas are on meters. The bathroom and toilet are one flight down. Mr Ducker and I provide the light bulbs, but not the loo paper. It's best to keep a roll by your door. And of course you're expected to keep your room tidy, and to clean up after yourself after you've had a bath.'

She handed the girl a Mimeographed sheet with five provisos. They were boxed for emphasis:

> NO CANDLES
> NO PETS (THIS INCLUDES TURTLES AND FISH)
> NO CHEQUES
> NO MALE SUITORS AFTER 11.00 P.M.
> ALL RENT TO BE PAID IN CASH A WEEK IN ADVANCE

'Have a good look at that before you put your name on the dotted line.'

The woman folded the sheet and then the money Elkie gave her; it disappeared into a pocket among the pagodas. 'You might not know it being a foreigner, but there's the Heath at the back and nice shops just down the hill. Once you've lived here a while, you'll find it hard to move. There's your receipt. Mr Ducker will bring you a proper rent-book when he's up.'

After the landlady had gone, Elkie went down for the suitcase she'd hidden behind the wall and then ran upstairs, two at a time. She was happy, happier than she'd been since Pellipar. She was in her own flat, a flat she'd found herself, and after all the unspoken things that had happened between her and Helen Doran, she knew she had made the right decision.

'Where are ye going?' she had asked when they arrived at Euston Station.

'To call Helen. To let her know we've arrived.'

'Who's Helen?'

'You'll be staying with her.'

She tugged at his overcoat. 'I don't know any Helen. Don't be teasing me. You are teasing me, aren't ye?' But she knew by the shape of his mouth that he wasn't. 'Sure, didn't I run away with you? I'm your lover. I'll be staying with you in London.'

Running away, he thought, anyone else would have known it was a bloody joke. He looked at her standing there, clutching the handle of her ancient bag. 'Here,' he said irritably, 'give me that, and stop being silly. You can't stay with me. I never said you'd stay with me. If my mother hadn't been there—'

But she didn't hear the rest of what he was saying; she was still hanging onto the last words that he'd said.

She watched him walk ahead carrying both their cases and thought that she was dreaming, thought that his coldness in the cab to Belfast and then the boat-train would end, that it would end when he was home.

She sat in the cab with her hands pressed between her thighs. It rained that night and the drops fell, exploded, ran in slivers down the glass. She sat close to him trying hard to control her eyes, her hands, watching the neon lights smear the slick streets of the city that she had hoped would be welcoming, that she had hoped would be home.

'Who is this Helen?' she finally said when the cab stopped. 'Just who is she?'

'Helen was my governess. My father's mistress.'

'But I don't know her, Ivan. I'm no good at talking to people I don't know.'

'Would you stop snivelling? I can't stand women who cry—' He didn't finish what he was saying because Helen Doran was waiting to welcome them at her door.

The first thing Elkie noticed about her was her flame-red hair; the second was a sign tacked discreetly on the inside of her tallboy door. It was a Venetian proverb about guests and fish. According to the sign, guests and fish are alike because after a few days they both begin to smell.

Elkie threw the suitcase on the bed and unpacked: three dresses, two skirts, four sweaters. Coat, raincoat, nightgown, robe. The Duckers' giant wardrobe still looked empty.

She closed the orange curtains and began to explore. She opened all the drawers in the sideboard. She pulled the lining paper out and underneath found hairpins, some beads from a broken necklace, an old letter torn in quarters. She fitted two of the pieces together: *I don't know why this had to happen. I thought you* (illegible words) *I fall in love quite easily. Why . . .* The ink-letters faded into one another.

In the cupboard was a stack of plates: white, pink, blue. Plates with plaited wheat, daisy chains, tea-roses. Cups without handles, cups without saucers, wooden spoons, dull knives.

A stained towel, a womanly mattress beneath the bed. She flopped on top of the blankets grinning, thinking of the last time she'd seen him. It had been the night before the fight with Helen.

They'd had a bath together; she poured water over his head. How funny he looked, like she looked the second time he'd found her at the avenue, half-drowned like a rat.

She told him he was red as a lobster, and he said he used to spear lobsters on his summer holidays in Donegal. He had speared lobsters to earn pocket money and a woman at the harbour restaurant had bought them for the tourists. The woman had warned him to bring her only the lobsters he'd speared between the eyes because people ate the thorax, and they paid good money to eat it, and they didn't want to see it cracked.

And she slid beneath the water like one of those lobsters, and held her breath so long that he was frightened, so frightened that he pulled her up.

And then he dried her and they lay in bed only under the sheet. 'Kiss me there,' she'd said. 'Open wider,' he'd said, 'wider.' They had lain awake all night.

She had sent a letter to him care of Helen Doran three days ago with her new address. A sink full of dishes, scallion tops she'd dropped lay mashed on the floor. On the window-ledge the plants were dying. Only a rubber plant remained green and shiny; its waxy leaves drooped downwards.

She went to the Heath and wandered for an hour. The coots

flew close to the water, slowing themselves with their webbed feet as they skimmed the surface. They had not mastered the art of landing.

She thought of her dog and what her parents had written, that after she'd gone, Benjo had cried at night. He had never cried at night before.

And then of Ivan's dog, Flash, the old retriever, who had lived only for the day he'd come home. Flash was a gigolo. The bitches in the neighbourhood had licked his red bastards. He would wander; he would sometimes wander as far as Ballykelly to deposit his seed in another dancing young bitch.

She had sat by the window and prayed he would come. He would not come. If she wore this and did that he would come. If she pinned up her hair with permanent-wave clips and put fresh garlic in her soup. But he would not come. But if he came, she would tell him of her walk in the park. It would fill the silence between them like he filled her, for a time. He would go away.

She had gone to the hill to watch the children fly kites and had met a man who played the mouth organ and lived with his mother. He told her his name and how long he'd worked for the Parks Department. His knuckles were very hairy and she imagined the rest of him was, too.

He invited her into his hut for coffee and when she was inside, he still wore the hat he'd been wearing outside, a hat with a flattened top and a wide brim stained round the crown. It had two leather thongs that bounced against his throat. When he finally took it off, he apologized and shocked her by adding, 'I'm sorry, I don't have much hair.'

It was a cold autumn afternoon and the windows of the Nissen hut steamed up while the kettle boiled, while he played those sad and lonely songs. She was frightened sitting in his hut with the kettle boiling and the windows clouding over.

He used powdered milk in the coffee although there was a bottle of fresh milk on the table. 'Hard to meet people,' he said, and then she knew she wasn't the first girl to sit uncomfortably in a Parks Department folding chair listening to him say, 'it's hard in a city,' watching him pull nervously at his beard. 'Do you have a boyfriend?' he asked and she answered too quickly, 'Yes.'

He sighed. 'A pretty girl like you. It's hard when you live with your mother and you're my—' He did not say the last word, and she watched him pick up his hat, tip it forward, and put it back on his head.

She balanced the cup nervously on her knees; he stood up and wiped the windows with a cloth. His trousers were black and the seat of them shiny, his buttocks round like moons. 'You can see out now,' he said, and she was grateful he'd noticed that she was afraid. She said she must go, the wee cup of coffee was grand.

'Maybe,' he said, 'I'll see you again. You like kites. There's a man that flies Chinese kites on a Friday. We could come back here for a gin and tonic—'

'I must go,' she'd lied, 'my boyfriend's coming by.'

But he hadn't come the night before, or the night before that. And that pie uncut on the stove, carefully fluted and filled with apples and sliced almonds. She could throw it away.

She knew the reason he didn't come. Because of the note she'd sent to Helen's three days ago. It said: *Oh Pookie, I love you so.*

She was his rainy-day lover. Rainy day. She would go to hell. 'But there's no such place as hell,' he'd told her, 'only this.' So she'd go to Moscow and watch the changing light on the façade of St Basil's Cathedral. She would never go to Moscow. So little light. So little light in the world.

And she thought of the dinner that night at Pellipar House, and wished she'd been too drunk to remember that story his mother had told her about Flash. His mother had said that Ivan's old retriever had lived for the day he would come home, for the day he'd come back from England. How Flash had patiently waited, lived on and on past his natural life, and then had finally died, without ever seeing him again.

*

‘I wasn’t expecting you tonight, Ivan,’ she said, taking the paper cone of roses from him. ‘It’s over two weeks. You didn’t ring and say you were coming.’ She put her unprepared mouth up to his. He turned his face to one side to avoid her lips; the stubble of his coarse beard grazed her.

He went up the stairs, two at a time, and waited for her at the door. She unpinned the key fastened to her housecoat pocket and let them into the room. He threw his coat over a chair. ‘You really must find another flat. This one is so—’ ugly, he thought and turned away.

‘But I just found this one.’

‘Well it’s not exactly Buckingham Palace, is it?’

‘Of course it’s not Buckingham Palace.’ She looked quickly around the room to see what it was that had so offended him, then decided it must be the drooping plants on the windowsill. ‘You know,’ she said, ‘I wish I was good with plants.’

‘It would help if you’d water them.’

‘I do! But just lately I can’t seem to make myself do anything.’

He looked at her unwashed face, her dirty hair, and realized why she couldn’t take care of those house plants he had given her: she couldn’t even take care of herself.

‘Look,’ he said. ‘This room. Even a coat of paint would help. You shouldn’t live in a place like this.’

She started to say, I don’t want you spending any more rent on me than you already have to, but he was naked, lying crosswise on the bed.

‘Are ye going to stay the night, Ivan?’

‘I can’t.’

‘Why? Why do you bother to come at all? You never spend the night any more. You always creep out in the middle of the—’

‘Look,’ he said, raising himself onto his elbow, ‘this bloody room is suffocating.’

It’s not the room you’ve come to see, she thought, is it? She sat on the bed beside him and lifted her hair away from her neck. She knew that she would beg and that, later, she would hate herself for it. 'Please stay, Ivan. Just this one night. Please, *please*.'

'I have work to do. I have to go to Geneva tomorrow night.'

'Ge*ne*va.' She stared at her blue shoes, a row of nascent moons cut out across the toes. 'Geneva your high-class hooer?' she mumbled.

'What did you say?'

'Nothin'. I didn't say a word.'

'It's the truth, Luz. It's only for ten days.'

Her face vacant, sad, a Modigliani gypsy-woman portrait. 'Ten whole days till I see ye again.'

'Tell you what,' he said. 'When I get back, I'll take you out on the Serpentine. Would you like that?'

'Oh will ye, Ivan, will ye? In one of them funny, white boats with paddles?'

'They're called pedalos,' he said, and laughed. 'Promise.'

'That'd be brilliant! Out with you in a pedalo! Wouldn't I be the envy of Dungiven?' She reached down, low, and touched him. 'Won't you stay then? Won't you stay the night?'

'I've already told you I can't.'

'Not even if I wear my new nightgown?'

'Let's see it on you then.'

She went into the kitchen off the main room and returned with her arms spread wide, turning slowly once for him to see. A red rose on her pale shoulder. She was as naked as a doll.

'May I have this dance, m'lady?' He bowed low and then held her, an arm around her waist, and they waltzed, they waltzed decorously, around the crowded room. 'With whom do I have the pleasure of dancing?' he said in a baritone voice, 'is it perchance the woman that is the talk of all Moscow, the beautiful Madame Karenina?'

'No!' she said, pretending to be offended, 'You're waltzing with the Princess of Castille. Luz to you, Count Vronsky.'

'Yes, Princess.'

'Can we go slower?' she said, moving closer to him.

And so they danced in the darkened room, he seeing each discoloured wall, the window, the bed. He held her as though she were a doll.

She leaned against him, her head against his chest. She pressed her body against his and felt him pull away. She knew that it would do no good to protest. She knew he'd leave her that night, that he would go, and all she'd have then were the carved teak elephants that he had given her: two north, two south on the ivory window-ledge. With each turn she saw them under the dead plants, their trunks raised as if to trumpet, but they, too, were silently swaying.

Next door she heard the audio typist getting ready for work. Last night after Ivan had gone, she'd heard the typist and her lover. She'd heard them together and then she'd heard him leave. Loreen's door had slammed and then she'd heard her crying. Their headboards were against each other, like mirror images, on opposite sides of the wall. Loreen had cried on one side and she'd cried on the other. They'd keened loud enough in chorus, loud enough to wake the day-old dead.

The audio typist was tall and slim and wore Carnaby Street dresses. She had an embroidered dressing gown that Elkie envied. It was made of shantung silk. That one she saved expressly for her lovers' visits; the second she hid under her pillow, a shapeless cotton one she wore when she was alone. Loreen was alone most of the time. She'd met Loreen after she'd knocked on the door late one night for ice cubes.

'Never get involved with a married man,' Loreen had said. 'That's the one thing I said I'd never do and look at me! "It's over," he says. Just like that.' She snapped her fingers. ' "What do you mean?" I says to him and he says, "I mean just what I said. It's over. Kaput. Finished." And I says, "You mean to tell me you're ditching me, Martin? What the hell am I gonna do? I love you." And you know what that sod says to me then? "You'll get over it in a week or two." That's what that sod said. "A week or two," like it was the flu or something. It's been six months. Six long, bloody months jumping out of my skin every time the flippin' phone rings.'

'But who was it I heard ye with a few nights ago?'

'That chipolata!' She held up her little finger. 'I'm not going to be a nun, am I? Have to have a sausage every now and again so the hole doesn't grow together. How about your friend, the one I hear you with. He's not married, is he?'

'Oh no. Ivan's not married.'

'You're smart. Six bloody months.'

After she'd left with the ice, Elkie lay on the bed and wondered if Loreen looked as bad as she did when she'd been crying. She must, she thought, she's a blonde. Blondes always look terrible when they cry.

And she had slipped down the straps of her gown and lain back on the bed like a statue of Niobe, or the firm-breasted figurehead on the prow of some ancient sailing ship.

Loreen sat on the end of her bed. 'You say your friend's over thirty? You've got to excite them that little bit more when they're older, love, otherwise they lose interest. I mean Martin's wife was dead boring. With her he was nothing but a missionary man.'

Loreen stubbed out her cigarette. 'Take a whiff of that, Elkie.' She lifted her wrist. 'Shalimar. Bought it for me in the Harrod's Sale. And I thought my ship had come in. Well, it did for a year.' She giggled. 'Came to port twice a week when the wife was at bingo.'

'What exactly did you do to make him . . . to keep him interested?'

'Well, a few Chinese positions, fishnet tights, that sort of thing, you know?'

'No.' Elkie blushed.

'Ask him what he likes.'

'I can't.'

'Why not?'

'I can't. I just can't.'

'We was all from Greenland once, Elkie. You've got a tongue. Just ask him.'

'Loreen, he doesn't talk when . . . when we're together. He doesn't say much anyway, but when we're in bed he doesn't say anything.'

'What about books? Ever look in books?'

'It's no use! He never wants to stay the night any more.'

'I know! Mouth music! That drives most men mad.'

'I can't read music. How can I learn to play a harmonica—'

She shook her head. 'No, no, love. I mean . . . you know, *soixante-neuf*.'

Elkie bit her lip, turned red.

'Look, love. You just need some atmosphere here. He's not the sort of bloke who's used to girls who live in bedsits. We'll go to Debenhams and buy a nice shade with a fringe for this lamp, get a vase for some flowers. Then we'll walk down to Soho and buy you a G-string and some black stockings. Did you ever think about straightening your hair?'

'Me hair? What's wrong with me hair?'

'It's not the style. Girls in my office iron their hair to make it look straight.' Loreen handed her a mirror. 'Have a good look at yourself. You're too clean, too scrubbed—'

'Too plain.'

'Jesus, Elkie, you're not plain. You're provincial. Try and think of yourself as exotic. What's the most exotic thing you can think of?'

'I used to think circus people were exotic. They'd come into me da's shop and ask for things we'd never heard of, like Jerusalem artichokes.'

'That's not exotic! Exotic is like them pictures in the mags of all them ladies in slinky, black dresses laying against grand pianos and smoking cocktail cigarettes. Like this.' Loreen sucked in her cheeks and leaned seductively against the wardrobe, her head thrown back, the line of her arm broken at the wrist. 'We'll paint some stuff on your eyes, add a few pillows here and there, and . . . bingo! Your bedsit's a real boudoir!'

Loreen picked up Elkie's comb and pulled her hair backwards. 'You should wear your hair off your face, combed back all sleek-like.' She looped her hair into coils and pinned them flat against her head. 'Christ, what a difference! Makes you look ever so sophisticated.'

Elkie stared into the mirror, watching:

The first time it wasn't like this. It was so simple. He held me against him and kissed me till my toes curled and I could hardly breathe. And there was no talking then, but it didn't matter, and he guided my hand and I touched him where he wanted me to. I was afraid, but I wasn't afraid. I saw that beautiful dress and my shoes on the floor. It was all that sherry. I was reckless with the sherry.

He touched me where I had never been touched before and I let him. I wanted him. I wanted him more than anything. I said, 'Won't your mother hear?' and he said, 'Mother planned this. That's why she let you wear that dress. Come here, princess. You're on the far side of the bed. Is this your first time?'

I said, 'Yes,' but I lied. My first was that soldier-boy who got me drunk on Marsala and, because I knew there wasn't going to be any blood, I thought I'd better tell him I rode Percherons. Sweet Jesus, I'd never been on a horse in me life.

'You're cold,' he said, and got up to close the curtains. He was as naked as a jaybird. Six times that night and three times in the morning. And when I got up it ran down my legs. 'We'll have to run away together,' he said that night, 'now that you're a fallen woman.'

And I answered him, 'Yes!' before he had the time to reconsider. I was already on the *Orient Express*. I'd only read about it, like Anna and Vronsky, but I wasn't leaving Seriozha behind, just my old, green bicycle.

Me da never approved of me reading that book, said it would put a thousand devils in me. I read it the first time when I was sixteen. I must have read it a dozen times since then, stumbling over the names till I had them clear in my head.

Anna was my nickname; mammy called me that to tease me.

And more than anything I wanted to get out of Dungiven, to see the world, to go to Moscow and St Petersburg. Mammy'd say, 'Why don't you go out and do something instead of reading that old book? You've read it before. Jesus, the pages are falling out.'

Vronsky, Count Alexei Kirillovich Vronsky. I always knew that one day I'd meet someone like him, tall and handsome, that somehow he'd find me and take me away from Dungiven. And so when I saw him in the middle of that field, it was fate that was smiling down on me. I knew the man standing there, sure I'd known him for years. I even heard myself say, 'Vronsky!' just under my breath. He looked just like what I'd always pictured he'd look like.

And I picked up the book the other day, just to see what it was like trying to read it again, and Ivan asked me why I was crying, and I couldn't explain. Something had happened. Nothing was the same any more . . .

Loreen said, 'Your eyes are watering, lovey. Am I pulling your hair too tight?'

'No,' she said. 'Just keep combing, Loreen.'

'Now if I'm hurting you, you let me know.'

And Elkie smiled; she smiled with half her face.

8

Mornings when I wake too early.
There is a dead light in the room.
Tom Paulin, 'Before History'

It's bright outside today, but I can't make myself get out of bed. I just lie here and stare at the elephants on the windowsill. Still no money from mammy though I wrote over a week ago. And when it does come, there'll be the usual lecture about marriage and respectability. I'm not a nun. I won't be a nun. I want to be like Anna who doesn't give a damn what people think.

He says he feels guilty about taking me away from Dungiven. He's been paying for everything. I can't ask him for any more; I'd rather starve. I can live on almost nothing if there's just the rent.

Loreen's gone to work and it's quiet. I'll stay in bed and read. He only comes at weekends now, and I have the whole of the week to get through somehow. If I can just make myself roll out of bed, roll onto the floor, then maybe I can make myself get up.

We went to a ball last night in Henley. I pinned a pink carnation behind my ear. We ate dinner on the river and there were lanterns hung in the trees. I wore the sleeveless black dress Loreen'd lent me. The oxters were too low and I was worried that people could see my slip. Loreen didn't have a black petticoat so I had to make do with my white one.

We ate beluga caviar and avocado pear with dressing where the stone was. An old man came to our table and asked me to dance. He winked at Ivan and said, 'Do you mind if I deprive you of this young lady's company for a while?' and Ivan just smiled. 'Not at all,' he said, 'be my guest.' It was the first thing he'd said all evening.

And while we were dancing, the dirty devil kept rubbing himself up against me. 'What lovely hands you have,' he said, like I was Little Red Riding-Hood, all the while trying to have a good look down the front of my dress.

His hand kept creeping lower and lower down the ditch of my back, and I kept pushing it up. I pressed my elbows against my body. He must have thought I thought my oxters smelled because he said, 'Don't worry, my dear, you smell enchanting.'

As we twirled around the floor I manoeuvred him to where Ivan was sitting. He kept saying gooey things like, 'It's an enchanting evening with the sun over the river like that, don't you think?' as though enchanting was the only adjective he'd ever learned. Every time he nuzzled me I screwed up my face like a fishwife. Ivan says I look like one when I do that. Ivan thought it was hilarious. He was laughing so hard he nearly fell backwards in his chair. Jesus, I could have strangled him.

The minute the band stopped playing I ran back to the table. 'You handled that badly,' Ivan said, 'rushing off like that. Now he really feels like a rake.'

'I don't care if he feels like a spade. I don't give a damn what he feels like. I didn't ask him to dance.'

He looked at me, then looked away. 'Your hair's coming down. You look a mess. Why don't you go and comb it.'

I touched the back of my neck. Ducktails were swimming down. It was that old bugger. But I didn't tell Ivan that. That old bugger had tried to put his fingers through my hair. My neck went stiff as a board. So I stepped on his foot. I thought it'd be less noticeable in a crowd than belting him in the stomach. He shouted and limped for a while and I thought what a crybaby he was; I'd only stepped on his foot. He looked embarrassed for a moment and then said, 'Gout. Gout's been bad lately. Big toe's gone to hell.' He pinched my cheek. 'Aren't you a sassy little thing? For a wallflower you've got a lot of spunk.' I was still thinking about what he'd said when Ivan told me to stop my bloody day-dreaming and go and comb my hair.

In the bathroom there were mirrors everywhere. I leaned right up against the glass and stared at myself. I couldn't believe it was me in that beautiful dress and my hair all done up. An hour Loreen'd worked on me. The *pièce de résistance* was the cloth carnation behind my ear.

I turned sideways to the mirror and lifted my elbows. Damn slip would have to be white. Loreen said she never wore anything under this dress. Not a stitch. Said it really got the men going when she told them that. Wish I'd had the courage to do it. I was sick and tired of having to keep my arms plastered to my sides.

I turned in front of the mirror like a music box ballerina, as slowly as when mammy used to hem my skirts: feet together, shoulders back, mammy shooting the chalk powder from the rubber bulb. Like when she hemmed my yellow dress that time so's I could go to my first ball.

'Cinderelly,' she'd said, 'all dressed in pale yelly, don't you spill anything on this dress, and you be home before midnight or your da and I will be roaming the streets looking for your pumpkin coach. Now hold still, will ye?'

'I can't! I can't, mammy! I'm too excited!'

'And don't let them boys at the Castle get too close to you. You keep your distance.'

'Oh mammy!'

'You're still only a wee lump of a girl. I know what goes on at them dances. And don't you dare sit in the back of the coach with any of them boys.'

'Why not?'

'Just.'

'Just because what?'

'Just because it's a mineral in the hand, and then a hand up the knee, Elkie. I know what I'm talking about. You just do as I say.'

At my first dance I didn't dance once. I sat on the platform with my stiff, yellow skirt spread out all around me and watched everyone else.

It wasn't as though no one asked me; a couple of boys asked me for a turn around the floor, but I'd made a promise to myself that I wouldn't dance with anyone except Jimmy McDowell. I was dying to dance with Jimmy McDowell. I had a secret notebook where I'd written down everything I knew about him: the date of his birthday, the foods I'd seen him eat, the licence number of his father's yellow car. Every time he danced with some girl I followed him all around the floor with my eyes.

Dear God in Heaven, I prayed, please let him ask me to dance. I'll never do anything bad again. I won't touch myself, and I'll go to church every Sunday and give all my pocket money for a whole year to the black babies in Africa if only You'll make him dance with me.

My eyes were closed in prayer when he finally walked over to where I was sitting by myself and said, 'Nice dance, Ethel Wallflower.'

I beamed at him. The taffeta swished when I stood up. I put out my hand so he could lead me onto the dance floor. He just laughed and swaggered back to the other side of the floor with his mates.

I was flummoxed. I didn't know what a wallflower was. I thought it was something nice, like a buttercup, like the colour of my dress. The first thing I did when I got home that night was to get out the big, old dictionary. It said a wallflower was 'a pale yellow or brownish-red flower that clings, wild, to the sides of walls – and someone who chooses not to, or is not chosen to, dance; a spectator.' I cried all night and wouldn't eat the next day.

Elkie made a face in the mirror. 'Damn you, Jimmy McDowell,' she said. 'Haven't thought about you for years. It was that old devil that made me think of you.' "For a wallflower you've got a lot of spunk." Spunk. I never think of myself as having any spunk. Don't seem to have any with Ivan. I never say a word out of line to Ivan; I only scream at him in my head.

"Why don't you go and comb your mop," as though I was a skag because I had a few ducktails! Damn ye! There's nothing wrong with me. It was that old bugger who started running his fingers through my hair.

And how dare ye ignore me all evening! Talking ballet and opera with them bloody bankers as though I wasn't sittin' there. 'Damn ye, Ivan,' she shouted, 'damn ye, damn ye!'

She damned him in the bathroom, a hundred pairs of passion-pink lips damned him. She should have known. She should have known that night when she'd come to the house with her bag. When he answered the door, his mother behind him, she could tell he was shocked to see her.

'What are you doing here?' he said.

'I'm all ready to go with you,' she said, trying not to look too hurt. 'I'm all packed.'

'What?' he said, trying to wave his gloating mother away from the door.

'You asked me to run away with you. You told me to be here at a quarter to, sharp.'

And when he looked down the drive, the taxi (whose driver he thought had just pressed the bell) was only now approaching, and it was not Ivan, but his mother who had quickly picked up her portmanteau and walked with it towards the waiting car.

Thinking about that, Elkie leaned hard against the basin and closed her eyes. She started to sing, singsonging the rhyme she had jumped rope to as a child,

'Cin-der-el-la, dressed in yel-la,
Went up-stairs to kiss her fel-la.

Made a mis-take and kissed a snake.
How many doc-tors did it take?'

9

A wedding-cake face in a paper frill.
Sylvia Plath, 'Berck-Plage'

'So what did you do this week?' he said, glancing over her bare shoulder at the dancers.

She shrugged. 'What did I do? Nothing much. I can't remember. Didn't do much of anything.' Elkie looked into her lap and fumbled with the clasp of her bag. 'Oh . . . I had another letter from mammy. She wrote she'd bought a dress for the wedding.'

'Whose wedding?'

She slid lower into her chair in anticipation of his anger. 'Mine.'

'Luz!' He crumpled his napkin and threw it on the table. 'Why the hell did you tell her you were getting married?'

'Don't be mad at me, Ivan. I couldn't help myself. She kept sending these letters I couldn't stand to get, like if you really loved me you'd have asked me to marry you by now, and if ye had no intention of marrying me, then I was only smearing the family name by staying on in London. Ivan, don't look at me like that! I just thought . . . I thought that if I told her I was getting married, she'd leave me alone for a while. Her last letter upset me so much that—'

'That you lied,' he interrupted. 'That's what's wrong with you, Luz. Everything seems to upset you.'

'Don't you know that it's because of you that everything upsets me? Loreen says . . . she says you've changed me.'

'What does Loreen know? I haven't changed anything. It's

got nothing to do with me. Will you stop crying? I've told you before, I can't bear to be around women who cry.' He pushed himself away from the table.

'You're . . . you're a fish!' she called after him. He pretended not to hear her; he continued walking towards the pier.

The sun was going down; she watched the waiter go to each table and lift the lamp-chimneys until the wicks caught fire, and then replace each one again.

She took her mother's letter out of her bag and re-read it:

Oh Elkie, how happy your da and I are for you! This news is all we've been praying for! As soon as I got your letter I went to Londonderry and bought a dress for the wedding that I'd had my eye on. I got it at Austin's, and it's wild expensive, but your da doesn't mind. We dipped into the Post Office savings.

I'll describe it to you. It's made of organdie and has a Romany neckline and has a dozen seed pearls sewn on the collar. It's the colour of orange blossoms. I'm looking for some shoes to match. If I can't find the right shade (which I doubt), I'll buy some white cloth ones and have them dyed specially.

We hope you'll settle on a summer wedding so there's a chance of nice weather. We can have the reception at the Mission House. Nothing too grand under the circumstances. At least he's been decent enough to do the right thing by you.

Have you got yourself a wee job yet? You know you'll need to for all the little extra things you'll need to start off your home with. I know you're too proud to be asking him for money all the time . . .

The man she had danced with stood looking down at her. She refolded the letter quickly and returned it to her handbag. 'I see you're alone, wallflower,' he said.

She lifted her chin aggressively. 'My partner's taking a wee walk.'

'How about a dance then?'

She indicated his empty chair. 'Dance with me friend there. I'm sweatin'.'

‘So you want to play hard to get,’ he said, sitting beside her. ‘Have you known Ivan long?’

‘You know Ivan?’

‘There aren’t many people here who don’t. You don’t have to play the provincial with me. You know about his money. You wouldn’t be with him otherwise.’ He tried to cover her hand with his.

She jerked it free. ‘I don’t know what you’re talking about.’

‘I dare say you’re prettier than some of the ladies I’ve seen him with.’

‘What d’ye mean?’

He laughed. ‘Promise me a dance and I’ll tell you, wallflower.’

‘I don’t want to know then.’

‘Well,’ he said, ‘suit yourself.’ He stood up to go. ‘Some people can’t see the forest for the trees.’

‘Who’s he usually with?’ she asked, the tone of her question urgent now that he had turned away to go.

‘You haven’t promised me that dance yet.’

Elkie looked towards the river; he was walking along the pier. She sighed, relented, threw Loreen’s sequinned clasp-bag onto the seat of the chair.

Ivan stood listening to the water as it hit the small boats tethered to the pier. The smell of fish, summer, night. The pier at Raemore Head.

He and Flash would go down to the sea at dawn and take a fisherman’s boat, Flash guarding the bait can, he sculling with one oar. His father had taught him to row like that, to scull the short oar. The fishermen purposely left only one oar on board so no one could steal their boats.

The fat woman bought the fresh lobsters he’d caught for the harbour restaurant. ‘Don’t you be bringing me those, boy,’ she said, ‘those ones that are cracked.’

It was harder to spear them that way, the way she wanted, aiming at the head, between the eyes, the mackerel bait bringing them to the surface. Aiming the cane spear straight into the shallow water, pinning them to the bottom, then bringing the spear swiftly up.

He remembered the morning he had sculled back to the pier and his mother had been waiting for him. Flash jumped out of the boat and began to lick her leg.

She stamped her foot in anger on the weather-beaten boards. 'I've been half out of my mind worrying about you! Your Aunt Ethna wanted to call the police, but I thought you'd be down here! Who taught you that, stealing people's boats?'

She grabbed the bucket from his hand. 'There!' They watched the lobsters and the sea water make great arcs before they disappeared into Loch Foyle. 'Damn you, Ivan! You're just like your father! One day you're going to get your comeuppance. You've always had everything your own way and one day, life's not always going to be so easy.' And he stood there on the pier, twenty-five years later, thinking of the morning she'd been so prophetic because it was that winter his father had drowned, and he had been sent inland.

He started to walk back. He stooped to pick up a fishing line, a dead minnow still attached to the hook. He coiled it and threw it over the boathouse roof. He wondered who, long ago, had ordered the painting of the faded letters on its side. REPENT O SINNERS, it said in an impressive script, AND YE SHALL BE SAVED.

They swung in and out of the other dancers. Elkie said nothing, waiting for him to speak. She rested her chin on some invisible platform, watching the dull light flicker on his bald head. Her partner was the only man wearing a cummerbund.

'When can I see you again,' he asked, 'without Ivan the Terrible around?'

'How long have you known Ivan?' she said, repositioning his hand.

'Since he was a boy. I knew his father. We used to work for the same merchant bank. His father was English, you know.'

'Was he? But what about their estate?'

'The estate's from his mother's side of the family. Minor Northern Irish gentry. It's a pity James died so young, then again, maybe not. He was an unhappy man.'

'Why was he unhappy?'

'I think he was one of those people who were born unhappy. He used to say it was because his wife refused to divorce him. James had a mistress he was madly in love with, a romantic governess. Hasn't Ivan told you any of his sordid family history?'

The bedroom Helen Doran had kept locked: the pictures all around the tops of the table, the tallboy, the vanity, the floor. Pictures his father had taken of them with a time-release camera, smiling faces in a garden, stopped in time. 'Not much,' she said, 'he doesn't like to talk about his family much.'

'Like James. Never gave much away unless he was tight. Liked to get tight. He told me the wife had tricked him into marrying her. He never forgave her for that. They were engaged when Morgan Grenfell decided to send him to Hong Kong. He told her he'd be back in a year and they'd get married. She didn't believe him and pricked his French letters. The closest old James ever got to Hong Kong was a smoking jacket with an embroidered dragon I sent him for his first anniversary.' He laughed. 'I don't think he appreciated my joke very much.'

'How did his father die?'

'I don't remember, my dear.'

'You must remember if you were such a good friend of his.'

'All right,' he said. 'He drowned. The death certificate said Accidental Death by Drowning. Who am I to doubt the coroner? Besides, wallflower, like I said before, money talks. Money lies too.'

Water ran down the steep roof of the hotel by the river; water sluiced into the troughs of its cast-iron gutters. Dancers covered their heads. A cat, forsaking shelter, darted from beneath a dripping table. A pink cloth carnation lay in the middle of the waxed square of dance floor.

Elkie watched him as they got into the car. His thin lips, green cat's eyes, the habit he had of running the tip of his tongue between the corners of his mouth.

She thought about what that man had said, but she knew it had nothing to do with his money. She lay down on the leather seat and closed her eyes. She tried to imagine him in church, gladioli around the altar, her hand resting lightly on his arm. Do you take this man for richer or poorer. No. It had nothing to do with his money.

She remembered herself as a child, kicking the rope swing higher and higher, singing, 'Here comes the bride, forty inches wide.'

And now she made him kneel by the bed. 'Will you marry me?' he said, kneeling by the bed. He was so handsome.

Mammy had started her hope chest when she was a baby, had filled it with napkins and bed-linen. Handmade quilts, a toaster, silverware added one piece at a time: knife, fork, spoon, knife, fork, spoon. And it was still on the shelf. Can't be left on the shelf.

She was dreaming. Something old, something new, something borrowed, something blue. The bride was blue. The bride's mother wore black and the wide bride could have done with a size larger dress.

10

Cold glass, how you insert yourself
Between myself and myself.
Sylvia Plath, 'The Other'

I'm so happy. I never thought I could be so happy. I tell him so and he says, 'Don't be. To say it only means you'll lose it.'

Just the glow of the street light, we lie awake all night. 'Turn over,' he says and we do, facing away from the window. We don't sleep; we never sleep, wide awake all night. 'I don't understand it,' he says, 'I've always slept with other lovers.'

He wears a smoking jacket with wide lapels and deep pockets. He carries sweets in those pockets, rolls of peppermint candy. His breath is like mammy's after she's drunk mint tea, green specks between her teeth.

He gets into bed like a hurdler, one leg tucked up beneath him, holding the mints. 'Want one?' He peels down the tight, paper tube for me. My nails are too short.

His cock touches my leg. 'Your feet are frozen,' he says, 'warm them before you put them on me,' and I rub them together quickly; I am his cricket, his cockroach, his Niña, Pinta and Santa Maria.

We roll on the bed, clutching each other as though we are drowning. I blush. 'Kiss me there,' I say, wide on the bed, he looking up from Africa. I feel his beard slide along my thigh, my leg. Like monkeys we play, hiding in each other's fur.

I wait for him to say something and he says nothing. I get so frightened he'll get bored with me, wishing he was with someone else in a strapless dress and mandarin fingernails instead of in my little room with me.

I'm so nervous about not being able to think of something to say that I've started to write possible topics of conversation on my palm. I'm afraid one day he'll notice. What I want to say is what he does not want to hear. I want to say, 'I love you, Ivan,' but he would be afraid of that, so I pretend to scratch my nose. Above the lifeline, in faded blue letters, I see CIRCUS PEOPLE.

'You know,' I start, 'I used to think circus people were exotic. They'd come into me da's shop and ask for things we'd never heard of, like Jerusalem artichokes. I loved the way they smelled. Like their animals. While they were in Dungiven, they never mixed with anyone in the town. I liked that, the way they kept themselves apart, the way they wouldn't give anyone the time of day. I'd go down to the fairground to watch them. I liked the trapeze artists the best, flying through the air in those skintight suits—'

He'll be pulling on his trousers soon but. I've often thought I'd throw them out of the window. Then Mrs Ducker would have a real fit, rent in arrears and men's trousers impaled on the railing. Then he'd *have* to stay, all women in the building, not a pair of trousers to be had. But he'll go, pull on his socks, his pants, shirt last, ask me to button the cuffs. And if I'm lucky, a kiss. He doesn't like to kiss me. His lips are too thin; his mouth is too small.

Last week when he was putting on his shoes he said, 'When I have something, I'm not interested in it any more. It's the chase, the getting of it.' And that night I had a terrible dream, and in the dream we hadn't seen each other for years. I wanted to tell him he could have had everything, but I wasn't able to speak. He handed me a bag. I saw lights flashing and I didn't know where I was, only that I was trying to talk and no words were coming out. And then I took his hand and held it, longer than I should have, and he said, 'I'll never forget you, Elkie,' and then he ran away and didn't look back.

I woke up sweating and started slapping the bed. I turned on all the lights. I sat by the window. I put on some water and let it boil and boil. I wrote him a letter in steam on the window:

Dear Ivan,

You never stay any more. You come and then go, and I'm left to make sense of the walls. The others in the house hear me cry. When I pass them on the stair they look at me strangely. They know.

I don't want to go on like this, living from weekend to weekend. I was all right till I met you. But I can't go on like this. Mammy said a girl my age should be out enjoying herself, going to dances, having fun. She said, 'The world should be your oyster.' Well, I haven't had much fun. I'm too afraid of losing you. I'm more afraid of that than dying. Not to see you again, or smell you, or touch you. It would be like being dead.

You said that if something ever happened between us, you wanted to keep that picture taken when I was seventeen, next to mammy's washing line. You pointed to my face and said, 'You know, you've lost that. That look of determination.'

Oh yes. Yes. At seventeen I believed the world was my oyster. I wanted to wear yellow dresses and dance at the Castle with Jimmy McDowell. I wanted to ride the *Orient Express* and wave goodbye to Europe at the Dardanelles, to go to Moscow and St Petersburg.

And now I don't want to do anything. I just lie in bed and look at the plants and say to myself, 'When the light hits the top leaf of the rubber plant, I'll get up,' and an hour later, 'When it hits the baby elephant's trunk,' and then by that time it's noon, and I'm still in bed.

Not that I want to bore you, but the letters from home are getting worse, mammy asking if I've chosen my dress, sending clippings 'for ideas', as she calls them, from the *Londonderry Sentinel:* 'For her wedding the bride chose a white cotton gown styled with tucking in front and back and adorned with Cluny lace.'

I keep all her letters in a shoe box in date order. I'll pull one out now, like a rabbit out of a hat, and read it out to you: *So glad you're all moved, Elkie. By the way, are you married now? I am sorry to be so plain, but it's the only way I know to express myself. I do not care to beat around the bush or be like other people who're afraid to ever express an opinion. It seems so as he helped you to move, and you talk like you cook for him in this new flat. It seems you spend so much time together. If I were you and you were I, you'd be wondering the same thing.* Etcetera.

And here's a more recent one in a lighter vein: *Now the letter your da and I got today should have been written as soon as you felt that he was the one you were sure you'd spend the rest of your life with. If we'd got that one, then we would not have been writing you to come home for any reason, as your da and I were young once and in love, and we know that no one on earth could have changed our minds. Some people tried to keep us apart and come between us, and family wanted us to wait until the end of the war, but we did not and we have never been sorry. We would not have mentioned your coming back to Dungiven in any shape, form or fashion if we'd known his intentions towards you were truly honourable. So glad you want a long engagement. Your da and I were together for two years before we got married, and it was such a happy time as we did not have all the responsibilities of life, but had found each other and were so happy so now, in turn, we're glad for you. So send us a picture of him and yourself for the mantelpiece and bring him home at Christmas.*

I can't sleep at night, Ivan. I keep thinking you'll come even though you don't. I sit in a dress, one I've saved all week, crying bolt upright so's I won't wrinkle it. I won't even lay on the bed. Loreen says I'm mad, that you have to learn to let things roll off your back in this world. Well I don't know how to do that.

I don't even know how to talk to you. I start to say something I've rehearsed a hundred times and, when I start to say it, the words just dry up in my mouth. I've thought of running away, but that wouldn't solve anything. Not for me.

You've never loved anyone but yourself. You've never had to share. Your da tried to make you. I remember you told me he'd take you to Dr Barnardo's every year with all your toys except three. He didn't want you to be selfish. It's not his fault that you are.

I can hate you all I want, and the next Saturday you come, no matter what I've made up in my mind, that this time you'll surely be different, you take off your shoes, lie on the bed, stare at the ceiling-rose and your silence comes up from all sides.

I sit by the window and watch the world go by. One day I saw a dead sparrow on the ledge. It had fallen out of its nest. The dull feathers weren't even feathers, just down, its tiny, yellow beak pointed to the sky. Rain ran down the poor dead thing's wee throat.

I stared at it for a week before I had the courage to ask you to pick it up. 'Please pick it up,' I said, 'I can't stand to see it there. It makes me too sad.'

And you swept it off the ledge. If only you'd picked it up for me, we could have put it in a cloth-lined matchbox and given it a proper burial in Mrs Ducker's garden. You couldn't understand. 'For Christ's sake,' you said, 'it's only a dead bird. Stop behaving like a child. You never even saw it alive.'

I started screaming and crying. 'Haven't ye got any—' but I stopped myself from saying it.

'Haven't I got any what?'

Feelings! I wanted to scream it and scream it and scream it, but I didn't. I just buried my head under the pillow because I didn't want you to see me like that. I couldn't have afforded to let you see me like that.

II SUMMER, 1967

Nearby, on the wet terrace of a café, a waiter was wiping the slabs of tables; a melancholy brigand hawking local lollipops, elaborate-looking things with a lunar gloss, had placed a hopelessly full basket on the cracked balustrade, over which the two were conversing. Either the drizzle had stopped or Fialta had got so used to it that she herself did not know whether she was breathing moist air or warm rain.

Vladimir Nabokov, 'Spring in Fialta'

11

Fathers and grandfathers are not understood. Lands are mortgaged. And in Baden, there is roulette.
Anna Akhmatova, 'Northern Elegies'

Ivan went to Cabourg each year. Each time he walked up the Avenue de la Mer he saw the face of the Grand Hotel as he would a friend, a little older, a little changed.

At the hotel he could lie all day in his room; he could remain an outsider. In September he could order a plate of *chaudfroid*, the *maître d'hôtel* not protesting, 'But monsieur, that was on the summer menu.' Instead a red-boleroed waiter would serve the filleted poultry in jelly and withdraw.

He had first gone to the Grand Hotel in Cabourg with his father five months before he died. Helen Doran had gone too, to look after the boy. She had been twirling a new, cream parasol with flounces.

The first morning they'd eaten breakfast in the glass-sided dining-room which faced the Channel. She had thanked his father for the gift of the parasol; she had called his father James. The boy cried, 'He's not James to you!' and Helen had looked up from her plate in surprise. His father had turned towards the glass wall. The two adults on opposite sides of the table, tears on her face, the glass's reflection on his.

Twenty-five years later, in his son's jacket pocket, was a note he'd received the morning he left for his annual visit to France:

Ivan, I was quite surprised to hear that you are to be married! You could have had the decency to tell me. I am, after all, your mother. I wouldn't have known except for the enclosed which appeared in the Sentinel. *It was the thing to do as far as Pellipar is concerned, though I would have thought you could have found someone more in your league. Having said that, I did find her that night at dinner rather charming and, of course, quite beautiful. My congratulations to you both.*

He folded the note and engagement notice and returned them to his breast pocket thinking, Mother dear, you're not the only one she should have had the decency to tell.

He stood in the corridor of the train watching the Normandy countryside blur past. He pulled a Sobranie cigarette out of its wrapper, and then felt faintly ridiculous smoking a thin, red party-cigarette on a train. They'd been a gift from Elkie, a packet of cocktail cigarettes she had presented to him as a going-away present. He stared at the brilliant tube of tobacco thinking that it typified that quality of hers which both attracted and repelled him: her cunning (she'd said they would make him think of her when he smoked them), and simultaneously, her *naïveté*.

Elkie arrived an hour early at the Dives-Cabourg station. It was an old building with ornate girders and a high, domed ceiling. Wooden benches were pushed against the walls. She sat on one opposite the double doors which were fastened open in the heat. An old woman sat down beside her and began to eat plums out of a paper bag. She spat the stones into her palm and then threw them onto the floor.

Elkie watched the slow, mahogany clock and began to cry. She was afraid he would not come. The woman eating plums saw her and briskly moved away.

She went to a window to see if the train from Paris would be on time. The man behind the grill pointed to a timetable under glass and said something she could not understand. She bought a ticket from a machine and walked up and down the platform thinking he would not come.

Then suddenly the train was there, and people pushed past

her. The platform was almost empty. At the end of the train a woman struggled with a huge, bamboo birdcage then, beneath the empty temple, she recognized his shoes.

'Ivan! Ivan!' she shouted, running towards him, nearly knocking over the woman with the cage.

He was embarrassed to see her run like that, embarrassed when she grabbed his arm and put her face up to his. 'I've told you,' he hissed, still thinking of that engagement notice, 'no kissing in public,' and then turned away.

She stared at the empty tracks glittering in the sun. She felt like Kitty Shcherbatsky at the ball. When Vronsky had not asked her to dance, Kitty looked into his face and the look she gave him, so tender and full of love, Count Vronsky so callously ignored.

She waited for him outside the hotel. She stood by the revolving door between two laurel trees and stared at her bare left hand. She wished for a moment she had borrowed the ring. Loreen had said she was welcome to borrow it. 'It'd be so much less embarrassing for you, love. All them Catholic frogs knowing you're not married. You're welcome to use it.' But she had refused. There was nothing to be ashamed of. Nothing.

Ivan ran up the carpeted steps. 'The suite was ready for me when I arrived,' she said, taking his arm.

'I said it would be.'

'It's got a big, brass bed, Ivan. A really big one.'

'I know.'

'It's grand, Ivan,' but what she really wanted to say was, It's grand to see you again.

He pushed the bar of the revolving door. 'Silly girl,' he said, 'you aren't supposed to get into the same compartment as me. The one behind.'

'Kiss me,' she said. 'You haven't kissed me yet.'

'In the *room*,' he said.

In the foyer of the Grand Hotel the concierge shook hands with Ivan. He motioned to a bellboy to pick up his cases. The concierge tilted his head towards Elkie and playfully raised his eyebrows. Ivan threw back his head and laughed.

Their balcony looked onto the sea. Elkie stood at the window holding back the thin, net curtains. He lay naked on the floor, face downwards.

'In a few months there'll be snow,' she said. 'Snow,' she repeated looking over her shoulder. 'Just think of it. It's been a year of absurd weather.'

He sighed. 'It's been a year of absurdities. The weather's had nothing to do with it.'

She stepped back from the window and let the curtain drop. 'I want to go out.'

He rolled onto his back and covered his eyes. 'You go. I'm too tired.'

She stared at his bags at the bottom of the large, wrinkled bed. 'Ivan, if you stay here, I have to go through the foyer by myself. I hate to go through the foyer. They all stare at me.'

'It's your imagination.'

'It's not my imagination they're staring at. They stare at my clothes.' She held her skirt out like a fan.

'Then we'll go out and buy you some. But not now. I'm hot. I've had a long journey and I'm hot.'

She stared at her bare feet. The nail varnish was chipped. She wanted to say, And I don't even know how to ask for nail varnish remover because it's not in your bloody phrase book. 'If you're not going then,' she said, 'I bloody well am.'

His arm remained over his eyes. Before she left she knelt and thumped him, once, in the middle of his chest.

She walked across the gravel drive. She stopped for a moment on top of the mound of landscaped grass and flowers that the drive encircled and looked back at the hotel, so large and white like a block of uniced cake, and turned away again.

She walked down the Avenue de la Mer which was shaded with trees. Couples were sitting at pavement tables and laughing. Past the shops were houses. One had animals on its steep roof. She stood watching them as though they might suddenly come to life. Near the chimney was a nesting, glass bird and below it, a ceramic cat was positioned to look as though it stalked its feathered prey.

Seeing it, Elkie thought of the cat that sat beneath their table the night it rained on the river, the night he asked her to come to Cabourg.

He'd had turbot that night. After the waiter had put the silver chafing dish on the table, she lifted its lid. A dead eye stared at her from the Beaumarchais sauce.

'You never eat fish,' she said.

'I thought I would for a change.' He flaked the flesh away from the backbone with his fork. 'Why are you looking at me like that?'

'Because I thought you hated fish.'

'Luz,' he said, 'How would you like to go away for a few weeks, for a holiday?'

'That'd be brilliant! Where to?'

'To the *Côte Fleurie* in Normandy. It's a resort I visit every year, but you'll have to travel there by yourself.'

She thumped her fork on the table. 'I never see you but once a week and now you won't even—'

'No tantrums,' he said. 'I manage to get through a lot of paperwork that way. I'll see you off on the train and then I'll follow you two days later. The suite will be booked. You'll have *carte blanche*. Everything will be taken care of.'

'But what will I do with myself till you get there?' He had been furious with her when she'd asked him that.

She walked back towards the town along the promenade. There were shops along the seafront selling hats, dresses, chocolates. She stopped in front of the hat shop. A veil of yellow cellophane covered the window. She stepped into the shade of the blue-and-white striped awning and stared at the hats in the window.

Rows of guillotined heads sat on tiers of blue crushed velvet:

fruit-basket hats adorned with Carmen Miranda bananas, black lacquered hats, hats trimmed with silk flowers and antique velvet, bridal veils, sun bonnets, cloche hats decorated with feathers. In one corner she saw a card, High School English Spoken Here. It gave her the courage she needed to go inside.

Inside, the shop smelled of heat and glue. From behind the open curtains at the back of the *modiste*'s came billows of steam. A girl with a huge iron was pressing brims.

An old woman stood up behind the counter. She wore a black linen suit. Her mouth and cheeks were heavily rouged, her hair an even, raven's black. She said, 'A hat for you, *mademoiselle*?' and Elkie nodded her answer.

'Without a tape,' she said, 'you look like a fifty-three or fifty-four, but I check.' The proprietress measured her head with a rolled-up metre. 'Yes,' she said, 'your head is a fifty-four.' She chose a hat from the counter with a veil studded with black sequins. 'You like?'

'How much is it?'

'Four hundred and twenty-five francs.'

'Oh no, miss, that's more than I've got on me.'

Mme Deshouillers said, 'Well, how about this one?' She held up a pale cream hat with pheasant feathers on one side. 'This is very popular in Paris this season.'

'It's a lovely wee hat!'

'Three hundred francs.'

'I'm sorry, but it's more than I can afford to pay. I only have two hundred francs—'

'Don't worry your head. I know just the hat.' Mme Deshouillers leant into the shop window and picked up a Breton hat of unbleached straw; it had big, red flowers around the crown. 'We see how this one look.' She lifted Elkie's hair free of her collar and fitted it. The old woman clapped her hands together. 'You are such a lady in that hat!'

'And how much is it?' She was almost too afraid to ask.

'That one, let me see, he is one hundred and seventy-five francs.'

'A hundred and seventy-five francs. I'll take it!' Elkie took the last hundred-franc notes out of her bag.

'Is important for me that all my customers look beautiful. You look like such a lady in that hat!'

The waiter smiled at her as he dried the glasses. She had come to the brasserie for the past two days and sat at the same marble-topped table in front of the mirror. He had noticed her red hair and the curve her back made as she slumped into the seat, her shoulders hunched forwards. For two days she had read or written letters on blue notepaper, occasionally turning backwards to stare at her reflection in the glass.

She looked at the hat lying on the table and smiled. At least he'll like the hat, she thought.

On her table was a bottle of water although painted on the glass, in bright letters, was the word Ricard. Through the open doorway of the bar, she watched people running by in a sudden shower of rain. A couple huddled beneath the brasserie awning, their hair dripping.

The liquor burned the inside of her mouth and numbed her lips. The couple under the awning kissed. More Pernod, she thought, and less water, and in a little while I won't know if I'm standing up or sitting down.

She smiled again at the hat. She'd taken it out of the box to look at it. The price tag was still attached to the grosgrain hatband. She thought of the proprietress lifting a thin calf as she leant into the shop window for it. Elkie turned the tag over: 250 F. and she thought, But she didn't charge me that. I only paid a hundred and seventy-five. Dear God, she wanted me to have it.

The waiter brought a bottle to her table and smiled. 'Here,' he said, 'you try. Free. It's the speciality of the region for customers of three days.'

'What is it?' she asked.

'Calvados.' He poured some into two glasses. 'You wait for someone?'

'You could say that.'

'I finish soon. You like to make a walk with me in your new hat?'

She followed him down the steep bank. Flies were buzzing. Heat. Absinthe. Sitting on the damp grass beside him, she tried to remember how she'd got down the embankment or what she had said to him and couldn't. And when he took her chin and held it, she didn't pull away.

She said, 'Don't, please don't,' but by then they were lying in the grass. She rolled away from him. 'I shouldn't have let you do that. It wasn't right.' She sat up and brushed the grass off her skirt.

He laughed. 'You look like a nun, sitting like that. I never see anyone except a nun with a back so straight.' He imitated her and she smiled. '*Cabróna,*' he said, 'you look beautiful when you smile.'

'What's that word mean?'

'It's a bad word which mean little she-goat. You are a little she-goat.'

'Do you have a comb on you,' she said. 'Jesus, I must look a sight.'

He handed her one from his back pocket. '*Cabróna,* I want to make you hungry for me, but you are hungry for this other one. Will he beat you?'

'Beat me?' She started to laugh, a little too loudly. 'He doesn't give a damn anyway, so what I do or don't do makes no difference.'

He thought she looked so sad under her laughter, under her hat sitting slightly crooked on her head. '*Cabróna,*' he said gently into her cheek, '*Cabróna*, come here.'

A cluttered dinner tray had been left on the desk near the door. Ivan lay asleep across the bed covered only by a sheet.

The French windows were open. She walked outside, sat and looked towards the sea through the balusters. Ivan had said their pale, hourglass shape reminded him of bare Arabian dancers.

She noticed a book propped against the balustrade. It had a leather binding and gilt-edged paper. She picked it up.

It was a diary written in a large, bold hand. *Forced to make a disastrous marriage*, she read, *I must now pay for it for the rest of my life. I know what it must feel like to be an imprisoned man.*

The baby will be born in a few days. Every night Sarah presses my hand to her abdomen to feel the child kicking. She pretends to ignore my disinterest. She says that it will be a boy, 'A boy to make you happy, James. Only a boy can kick like that.' And then she smiles. It's her smile I can't bear, that and her cunning that in these last few months I have come so to abhor.

Elkie heard him change position and quickly put the diary down. She waited to make sure that he was still asleep. She picked up the book again and took out a photograph which jutted from the back pages. It was a sepia tint of a woman, a boy and a man standing in front of a glass house. The boy was crying, reaching out. Not to the mother who restrained him with one arm, but to the father who was walking away. Their shadows on the tall grass were short; the sun, unpictured, was going down.

12

On the balconies of the hotel, things are glittering.
Sylvia Plath, 'Berck-Plage'

'We must buy you some clothes today,' he said. He sat in a domed chair and pulled on his socks. 'And some shoes with a bit of heel. The ones you wear are too flat.'

Elkie sat on the edge of the bed, the sheet crumpled in her fingers. 'Hurry up,' he said, 'and get your clothes on. Gaby will be in soon to change the linens.'

After he said that she started, quickly, to dress. She wanted them to be out of the room by the time the maid came. She hated the way Gaby flirted with him so shamelessly, moved her head so light would catch the elaborate crystal-drop earrings which she wore. Yesterday she'd told her she looked like a bloody chandelier. Gaby, not understanding what she'd said, thought it was a compliment, and moved into the sunlight to make more rainbows on the wall.

Elkie went into the hallway to wait for him. She walked to the end of the corridor to a tall, leaded window above the landing. From there she could see the sand freckled with bright, beach unbrellas. It was there that they had their fight.

'*Bonjour, mademoiselle,*' Gaby said.

Elkie turned around sharply. To her irritation she saw she was wearing the chandeliers again.

'*Mademoiselle,* I have a question for you. Does Mr Ivan sleep well?'

'What business is it of yours?'

'I wonder. Because before he never sleep well when he come here. He always order champagne and oysters at two in the morning because he cannot sleep. For two. The kitchen wonder why he not want this year. But this is your first season with him. The one was here last year—'

'Shut up.'

Gaby cocked her head to one side, provocatively. 'The one was here last year had more fingernail than you.'

'What about the one last year? Tell me!'

Gaby slid both hands into the deep, front pocket of her fichu and shook her head. Elkie flew at her. 'Tell me about those oysters you fucking bitch—'

When Ivan managed to separate them, Elkie's right breast was bare. Gaby leant against a table, out of breath, out of reach, her beehive on her shoulders. She was gasping, wiping the blood from a cut on her mouth. 'You remember Pain d'Epice,' she threatened. 'You remember that I remember.'

Ivan turned to look for Elkie, but the long corridor was empty except for a pile of twisted sheets.

The slats of the Venetian blinds were almost closed. Beneath the window, narrow bands of light striated her shoes, the same low-heeled shoes her landlady had judged to be so respectable. Remembering that, Elkie unbuttoned her torn blouse and threw it to land over them.

She sat on the bed laughing; she cupped her scratched breast with her hand. Give them something to talk about in the dining-room, she thought, something besides the bloody weather.

She looked at the georgette dress hung over the top of the Chinese screen. She walked over to it in long strides, counting out loud to herself, 'Seven, eight . . . lay them straight.' She moved behind the screen and brushed the memory of the waiter and yesterday's embankment grass-heads briskly off her skirt.

She adjusted the lacquered panels to hide herself. She squatted, pulled her thighs to her chest. She sat surrounded, protected by six dragon legs.

Ivan stopped in the doorway of the bedroom, then walked to the basin and washed his hands. He dried them carefully, folded the towel, and put it on the rack to dry. On the other side of the bed he saw her toes beneath the Chinese screen.

'I think we need a walk,' he said addressing her feet, 'I think we need a long, long walk.'

The promenade was a mile long. The boards were fixed on to battens in the sand. A couple stopped in front of the *confiserie* not far from the hotel, and looked at the trays filled with marzipan fruit, foil-wrapped squares of bitter-sweet chocolate, the soft caramels that the resort town was famous for. He said, 'Looks like after what happened this morning, I'll need to buy the Princess of Castille something to sweeten her up.'

Two long, perpendicular counters were divided into small compartments; on the shelves behind them were hundreds of glass jars. The woman serving was corpulent; she panted as she tried to reach the jar of candied almonds. She weighed the sweets and then poured them into a white paper bag. He paid her and she slowly settled herself again on to her chair. A bell rang again when the door closed behind them.

Ivan picked up Elkie's hand and poured some pale green dragées into it. 'Did you know that Proust came here to write? He stayed at the Grand Hotel while he was writing *A l'ombre des jeunes filles en fleur*.'

Elkie, crunching almonds, walked stiffly beside him; she was bracing herself for what he would say. 'The concierge let me look at some old registration books to find out which suites he stayed in. He told me that no one could be sure because the Germans had renumbered the rooms during the war. You know,' he said, 'I like to imagine him walking on the promenade with that big moustache of his, like a Portuguese Jew's.'

'What's Portuguese juice?' she asked.

'You weren't listening to me, were you?'

'What does that mean?' she said, pointing overhead at the long banner strung over the promenade.

'*Fête de l'Eté* means summer festival. They have a carnival and a masked ball. People dance in the streets.'

She turned to him angrily. 'Oh come on out with it, Ivan! Say what you're gonna say! Didn't you hear those fat cows at breakfast this morning?'

'Did you understand what they were saying?'

'Jesus Christ, I'm not an eejit, you know. You don't have to speak a language to know that people are talking about you.'

'Because of that little episode this morning, I had to see the manager about Gaby's job. They were going to fire her.'

They weren't going to fire her. He had seen to it that they wouldn't. He and Gaby were accomplices, of sorts, because of something that had happened last summer.

Gaby had followed him to a small club called Pain d'Epice. It was on the harbour at the back of the town; its lights were covered with red shades. When he came out at one in the morning, she was outside the door smiling. He could still see her there standing under the street light, turning from side to side so that her full skirt would swing.

She stared at the boy with him. He was drunk and held on to his arm for support. He asked her why she was out so late, and she said she couldn't sleep. The boy chose that moment to lean against his shoulder and Gaby had said, 'Looks like you won't be able to sleep much tonight either.'

'All right,' he said. He blew up the empty bag of almonds and exploded it with his hand. 'So what was this fight about?'

'It wasn't about anything.'

'Come on, Luz. You started this. What was this fight about?'

'It was the things she was saying! She was saying you had oysters in your room and—'

'Oysters!' He started to laugh, relieved that Gaby had been more discreet than he had thought her capable of. 'Gaby was just trying to wind you up. Don't you realize she's jealous? You promise to steer clear of Gaby, and I'll buy you a dress, something elegant you can wear to the ball.'

He started to laugh again as he put his arm around her,

‘ “O Oysters, come and walk with us!”
The Walrus did beseech.
“A pleasant walk, a pleasant talk,
Along the briny beach:
We cannot do with more than four,
To give a hand to each.” ’

He pulled the dresses backwards on the rack. He handed her a long, black skirt and a red bolero with mandarin frogging. ‘Try this one,’ he said.

‘I don’t like it.’

‘It’s exotic. You’ll look stunning in it.’

‘Where’s the blouse?’

‘There’s no blouse. For the ball you’ll wear it without a blouse.’

‘But they’ll show—’ she called out to him. She looked at her clothes lying on the floor in the corner of the cubicle and then back at herself in the cheval glass. ‘Exotic is like them pictures in the mags of all them ladies in slinky, black dresses.’ As much as she disliked Ivan’s choice, she knew that Loreen would have approved of it.

‘Come out,’ he said, ‘and let me see you.’

The skirt fitted tightly over her hips, the slit in front came to the middle of her thigh. Along one side of the slit were fabric-covered buttons. The red bolero, cut square in front, just covered her breasts.

‘Here’s the hat that goes with it,’ he said. It was a tiny hat; it sat strangely on her thick hair. A black feather waved straight up like the arm of a wet man hailing a taxi in the rain. ‘Now you’re all set,’ he said. ‘You can go as Mata Hari.’

‘Who’s Mata Hari?’

‘A nightclub dancer who was shot as a spy.’

‘That’s great,’ she said, ‘just great. Why can’t I go as myself?’

‘Because it’s a masked ball. After the masquerade everyone reveals who they are, and then there’s a fireworks display on the beach.’

'Ivan,' she said, 'have you ever gone to this ball before?'
'Of course.'
'Someone you ate oysters with?'
'Would you stop thinking about Gaby?' he said. 'It shouldn't matter to you anyway.'
She stared at his reflection in the mirror, at the expression he now so often wore, wanting to see the face she had seen at the avenue, to see again the mask behind the mask.
She pictured herself that night in the dress and velvet hat with a black feather, passed from one pair of arms to another in a carnival atmosphere of revelry and licence. In their costumes and papier-mâché masks they would be hidden from each other legitimately. It was the sort of sport a man of deceit would love.

The carnival was held on the beach. Coloured lights were strung along the promenade. The light, whole in its necklace, blurred as it was reflected on the sea. Everywhere the smell of fried potatoes.
'Ladies and gentlemen, step right up. Don't push.' The barker jabbed his baton at the painted likeness of a bearded lady. 'This is no trick devised by the cunning of man, but a genuine freak of nature. And to my left,' he swung sharply to the other side, waving his baton at a red drop curtain with a Negro cupid, 'we have Black Aphrodite in all her naked splendour. She will perform a bacchanal the police have banned in Tangiers. Yes, Tangiers!'
Goldfish swam in bags of water, a costumed monkey sat in the oily glove of an organ-grinder. The monkey had a hat like hers, with one feather. It struck a tiny pair of cymbals, removed its hat and bowed. The crowd clapped, threw coins. Babies cried.
They stopped at a half-tent with busts of wooden clowns, their open mouths Venetian red. Mechanically they jerked from side to side, a carved frill around each neck, painted tears on flour-white faces. A boy was trying to throw a ball into their mouths to win a prize. Twenty clowns grimaced, shook their heads, screamed on and on in silence.

A devil passed her wearing a pointed hat and a stiffened beard made of yarn. His face and hands were reddened with ochre. He lunged at her with his spear and ran off, laughing.

'Why did you bring me here?' she said. 'I'm afraid.'

'Mata Hari,' he laughed, 'spies must learn to conquer their fear.' He grabbed her hand and pulled her with him. '*Deux billets*.' He threw the coins on top of the booth's counter, and the attendant swept them into a dirty box on his lap.

An urchin locked the bar into place. The huge Ferris wheel began to jerk, carrying them higher and higher above the sea, the jolting of the machinery swinging the seat.

At the top of the wheel the fairground was a blur of water and light. To frighten her, Ivan began rocking forwards and back, laughing, pushing his body, hard, against the bar. He forced their rusty seat higher and higher and higher. Elkie began to scream.

She pushed her way through the crowd. She could hear her heart above the barrel organ, the laughter, the screaming silence of the wooden clowns. She could forgive him for many things, but not for that, for frightening her like that in the swinging car. She ran from him, almost falling, towards the open stretch of beach. And as she ran, she felt like a freak, an oddity he was drawn to in some obscene way, like the Siamese twins or the bearded lady he had paid admission to see.

'Luz!' he called after her. He was drunk, drunker than she'd ever seen him. As he caught up to her, he threw his cigar into the sand and grabbed her, sliding his cold hand beneath the frogging.

'Get away!' she said, crying. 'You get away from me! You don't want me. You only want what you can pay for.'

The steam organ was wheezing Aphrodite's bacchanal. Elkie kicked off her shoes. 'You wanted a show,' she said crying, 'I'll give you a show.' And she began to dance around him sprawled in the sand, throwing her arms wildly, turning like a dervish, ignoring the small crowd of bystanders who had gathered around the bare-breasted dancer to watch.

They passed a man and his wife on their way to breakfast. Ivan smiled and the man moved his wife to the inside of the stair.

The Frenchman cleared his throat. 'You might like to know we hear everything that goes on in your room.'

Elkie pulled on his elbow. 'What's he saying? What's he saying?'

'Nothing. Be quiet.'

'And if you're going to entertain whores in this hotel,' he continued, 'you should dress them better.'

Ivan smiled and took her arm. 'What did he say,' she said, 'what did that man say?'

'That it's such a lovely morning we should have breakfast on the terrace.'

'That's not what he said.'

'Luz, he said the dining-room was crowded.'

'What you mean is that fewer people will see me, isn't it? Why don't you ever say what you mean? Why do you lie to me? I don't give a damn what these society people say about me. Why should you? If you cared for me at all—'

'Lower your voice,' he said, 'and when we get outside, I want you to take off that ridiculous hat.'

It was warm by nine, but cloudy. Half the tables on the terrace were in shadow. He chose a yellow table in the sun.

'These look like nuns' hats.' Elkie picked up a stiffly starched napkin. 'My girlfriend from down the road went to convent school in Portstewart, and her penguins had hats like this. They always reminded me of big, white boats. I used to ask Philomena did she think they'd float if you put them in the water—'

'Would you be quiet?' he said. 'I've had just about enough.'

The waiter brought a basket of rock cakes. Elkie kicked the bottom of the table after he went away, making the madeleines jump. He looked up from his paper. 'First the fight with Gaby, then last night, then that absurd hat you insist on wearing everywhere, and now behaving like a peasant at the table—'

The waiter crossed behind him with the coffee. He looked first at Ivan sitting stiffly against the back of his chair, and then at Elkie who stared at the gravel drive. It was then that the clouds moved, and they were cold now at their yellow table, for they found themselves, quite suddenly, in the shade.

They walked slowly along the tide line. The beach was covered with broken shells which cut into their feet.

Two men pushed a small sailing boat into the water and jumped on board. Elkie held the hat tightly on her head as she watched them working with the sail, the wind blowing the boat at angles from which it seemed impossible it could recover.

He said, 'For the last time, I forbid you to go back to the hotel in that hat.'

She turned towards him, her eyes squinting although the sun was behind her. 'I'll wear what hats I like.' She lifted the hem of her dress and waded out. She turned around to look back at him; he was rolling up his trousers. He waded away from her, out into the sea.

'Why did you bring me here, you bastard?' she said against the wind, against him, knowing full well that he could not hear her.

He waved for her to join him, and she climbed back up the steep, rock stairway. The promenade was empty now except for a few old men. They greeted each other by pulling on the brim of their flat caps.

They walked the length of the seafront. Only a few bathers remained. A man and a woman lay beneath a beach umbrella. As they walked past, the couple began to laugh hysterically.

Ivan's lips whitened as he stared at the straw brim. '*Now* will you believe me? Do you know what they're laughing at? They're laughing at that bloody hat. Now take it off.'

She walked away from him and locked her knees. 'No.'

'Take if off, Luz. I'm warning you.'

'You can go to hell.'

He lunged at her. She pulled away, but wasn't quick enough. He had already grabbed the hat.

They watched it bobbing on the water, the dye from the red grosgrain ribbon bleeding from the crown.

He started to walk ahead. He was feeling strange: ill, cowardly, victorious. But he could justify to himself what he had done. He'd protected her from herself. She had looked ridiculous in that hat. Donkeys in Sicily wore hats like that so the tourists would pay to take pictures of them, donkeys in picturesque hats to photograph with floppy, red flowers around the crown.

He wanted to apologize to her; he wanted to, but he could not. Instead he called back, 'Will you come now?' and from further down the promenade she turned from the sea to look at him, at his pinched and tired face and, for once, she knew that he was sorry.

They said nothing as they walked to the steps at the end of the beach. They were part of the retaining wall built to protect the resort houses from the sea. He sat down and took off his shoes and socks; only now was he beginning to think clearly.

It wasn't really the hat that had made him so angry; it was that engagement notice she had printed in the *Sentinel*. He had planned to ask her about it this afternoon. To put it under her nose and read it: *Mr & Mrs Francis Bonner of Dungiven are pleased to announce the engagement of their daughter* . . .

But it was not the right time now. The right time had passed. She had pushed him too far these last few days, and now there would be no more time. In the morning he would be gone.

She watched him move down the staircase, one step at a time, until the water covered his knees. She closed her eyes. She saw the stickers on his packing trunk. the rainbow prisms on the balcony wall, the cold way he stared at her, and how she wanted now to go under, the sea water numbing her, enchanting her. Pulling her quickly, swiftly, down.

13

In old Russia are fine ditches,
and in the gardens rotting summer-houses,
and the window glass is as black as an ice-hole.
Anna Akhmatova, 'Northern Elegies'

It's midnight. A train at eight tomorrow and he'll be gone. Something to do with stocks and shares. He didn't give me much time here, said that some deal had cropped up and that his work was more important.

I arrived two days before him because he'd insisted on travelling alone. He'd given me a map and *X*'d the places I should eat, the shops I should visit. He had arranged everything except the most important things.

He kept telling me stupid things like Proust came here to write. He said he liked to imagine him walking on the promenade with that moustache that made him look like a Portuguese Jew. I said I didn't want to hear about Portuguese juice. 'Where are you going?' I asked him. I imagined a map of Europe like the one in my old geography book: yellow for Holland, orange for Germany, pink for Switzerland. The cities he named lit up like small bulbs, and I connected them with a thick line moving eastwards.

I asked him, 'Is it because of the hat or my fingernails?' I'd hidden my hands in the folds of my skirt after Gaby had said, 'You can always tell a lady by the hands.' But he just turned away and wouldn't answer.

They never liked me at this hotel. I wasn't grand enough for them. The first morning I arrived, I was lying in bed and Gaby walked in with a big bowl of fresh flowers. When she saw me, the sheet pulled up to my neck, she said, 'There is mistake. This is the suite of Mr Ivan.'

'I know,' I said, 'I'm Mr Ivan's mistress.'

She dropped the bowl and kept saying, 'Sheet!' as she picked up the pieces of glass. She brought in another bowl and slammed the door when she left.

Ivan said he'd come here the first time with his father and Helen Doran. That one morning near the end of the holiday, his father had walked out into the sea, just walked out, and a fisherman had seen him and brought him in, half-dead.

He said his father had died that winter. Ivan had seen him in the greenhouse a few hours before he drowned. It was his mother who told him. She took him into the kitchen and gave him ginger biscuits and milk.

Their preacher was upset because his mother didn't wear black for the funeral. She said in front of everyone, 'I'll have you know, Reverend, I was a widow long before he was dead.'

After the whispering and the ginger nuts, he said he couldn't remember much except the wind snapping his mother's red dress. They came home together after the funeral and she gave him a glass of port. She left all the windows open and the snow blew in and the smell of turf and damp and the stink of the old hoof-glue factory from down the road.

I stole that picture out of his father's diary. It's an old sepia tint on Velox paper. It was taken in front of the greenhouse at Pellipar. His mother's looking away from the camera. The grass hides his parents' feet. They all look miserable, but Ivan's the only one that's crying.

He said his father was a great amateur photographer. He'd put the camera on the garden sundial and run back to stare into the box. He only smiled in pictures with Helen Doran. When I was staying with her those two weeks, she always locked her bedroom door, but one morning she flew out in a hurry and left it wide open.

I couldn't help myself. I went in, and in that room there must have been twenty pictures in different poses, all taken on the same day, in the same dress. Smiling faces in a summer's garden. Framed pictures on top of the vanity, the wardrobe, the floor. Pictures of James and Helen Doran taken with a time-release camera.

In a few minutes Helen came back because she remembered she hadn't locked her door. She found me in her bedroom and started to scream at me. She said that she'd never wanted me to stay with her, but she'd done it as a favour to Ivan, but Ivan or no, she wouldn't have me nosing around her things. Her past was her property, and for being such a nosey-parker I'd have to pack my bags and go.

I am going too. I can't walk around this bloody town any more on me own. I'm leaving tomorrow on the twelve o'clock. I hope I don't do anything silly like cry. God I hope I don't cry.

I'll write to mammy and tell her I had a wonderful time; I ate my first frogs' legs dinner. I can send my first telegram: *Ivan called away on important business stop still no date for wedding stop*

He said I was a seasoned traveller now, that I could get around on my own, and to prove it he bought a decal of the Eiffel Tower in a souvenir shop and stuck it on my bag.

Last night I slung the Mata Hari clothes over the balustrade. Ivan was asleep. They were hanging over the screen, all waiting to be packed. I don't know what came over me. There they were, lying in the sand. But I'll never understand why he threw my hat into the sea. He didn't know what that hat meant to me, or what it cost. He never knew the true cost of anything.

Before we came back to the hotel last night, we drank nut brandy out of glasses that looked like Easter lilies. He told me I drank too much. I said I drank to numb myself.

'What do you want to numb yourself for?'

I honestly think he didn't know. So I won't feel, Ivan, so I won't feel so much. But I never said that. I just smiled at him sweetly over the top of my glass. He would never have understood that. All he understood were foreign languages, and what knife and fork to use at dinner.

He held up his glass before we left the bar and said we must toast tonight. 'Chin-chin,' he said, 'chin-chin.' And I asked him what that meant and he said, 'Look it up when you get back to London. You must toast me now and say chin-chin.'

He's as slippery as a fish. I dreamt last night he was swimming under water, the sun dappling his skin. He's my fish. Teach me to swim, little fish. Teach me. I'll drown if you don't hold me up, out of the ice-white bath.

I wanted to tell him about Loreen, about how well the water rolls off *her* back. That Loreen can't stand waving at the window like I do. Her flat faces the back. All she can see are washing lines and overgrown gardens. That after her lovers leave her, I can hear her crying. Loud enough to wake the dead. That our beds are against the same wall, and she cries on one side and I cry on the other. And while I'm thinking about that, about me and Loreen, he says, 'Smile, Luz, I never see you smile any more,' and I say, 'Maybe I have less to smile about.'

Last night I watched his face as he came. He knew I was watching because he kept opening and closing one eye. And even when he came, he was silent. Afterwards he sat in front of the heater drying the bottoms of his wading-trousers. I switched it off and knelt between his legs, and butted his chest, hard, with the top of my head like a little she-goat.

Kneeling there, I thought of Lily Poston. Lily Poston's job in the town is to wash down the dead. She's the only woman in Dungiven to see everyone stark naked. Whenever I passed her on Main Street, I always used to think that one day Lily Poston's gonna give me a cold bath and I'm not gonna feel a bloody thing.

14

There's something desperate about trains . . .
What can be more fantastic, more desolate
Than the light of an electric lamp
Rocking in a small station at night?
Yevgeny Vinokurov, 'Missing the Troop Train'

It was after midnight. Elkie stared at her suitcase on the luggage rack. On the side was a sticker of the Eiffel Tower. Another suitcase stood beside it covered with names of far-away places. It was made of black leather and had gold buckles and stitched straps.

Her own cardboard case was dented. One of the catches didn't close properly, and on the corners the linen buckram had frayed. The iron tower tilted towards the handle. She had never even been there.

The woman who owned the expensive suitcase was a Dutch widow who had boarded the train at Cabourg. After Mme Smekens had introduced herself, she opened a box of chocolates. She ate the box of chocolates in front of her, and then offered Elkie the last square. Mme Smekens smiled, holding the box in front of her. She shook her head; the widow insisted. She took the chocolate out of its wrapper and put it in Elkie's palm. The chocolates dispensed with, she prepared for sleep; Mme Smekens removed her rings. 'I always worry that when I travel thieves will cut my fingers off,' she'd said. 'I never give them the chance.' The widow had smiled and folded her unadorned hands in her lap.

Elkie flattened the soft chocolate between her fingers. On the floor were foil wrappers. The widow snored again. Elkie reached for the bottle of wine she had bought before she boarded the night train to Paris. She was thinking of what the woman in the shop had said, that the wine was not expensive. She had noticed her battered case even though she'd tried to hide it. 'It's the local wine, *mademoiselle*,' she'd said, 'it's cheap but still quite drinkable.'

The lights in the corridor were shaking as Elkie walked to the dining car. 'You have no business going off like this.' She heard her father's voice in her head. 'No business, d'ye hear? For crissakes, you don't even know the man.' The lights in the corridor were shaking the way the hurricane lamp had trembled when her father had slammed the door.

The dining carriage was empty except for a man behind the counter. A glass case with hinged flaps covered plates of sandwiches and fruit. '*Quatre francs*,' he said, and drummed his fingers on the counter top, anxious to go back to sleep.

Elkie walked to the back of the dining car to eat her sandwich. The salt and pepper tray was bolted to the table. She shook it in frustration. 'You'll have to forgive your da his ranting and raving,' her mother had said, 'He's obviously forgotten what it feels like to be in love.'

And then her mother had said something which shocked her. 'When I was young, Elkie,' she'd said, 'I loved your da so much I would have died for him. Do you love like that?' And truthfully she'd told her mother, 'Yes.'

A few hours later Elkie opened her eyes to a dusty road running parallel to the track. The trees along the road were pruned like candelabra. The carriage was empty except for a sleepy Algerian who filled the china-blue bowls with sugar.

Mme Smekens liked her eggs soft. The yolk wet her bacon and sausage. 'Gorgeous, aren't they?' She pointed at them with the handle of her fork.

Elkie had never seen a runny egg before. She had always eaten hard-boiled eggs with yolks that flaked apart.

'This is what I adore about travelling,' Mme Smekens was saying, 'the breakfasts. I can't get my cook to make them like this. Indonesians are hopeless. They never manage to get the eggs right. And the scenery, of course. I adore the scenery from a train.'

There were mountains now, the colour of the sugar bowls, and fields of rye. Poles with sagging wire divided the landscape like frames of a film.

Mme Smekens mopped up the yellow juice with her bread and leaned over the vase of roses in the centre of the table. 'Very pretty,' she said, 'but I can never see yellow flowers without thinking of my late husband. He was an Egyptologist. The ancient Egyptians used yellow as their colour of mourning. He had a great respect for the wisdom of their culture and beliefs. He refused to have a yellow flower in the house.'

Elkie only half-heard her; she was thinking of a promise she'd made to her mother. 'Just a letter every week or so to let us know how you're getting on.'

The widow put her knife and fork side by side in the middle of the plate. 'I'd better not eat any more. That's the trouble with getting old. Horrible thing, dyspepsia.' She stood up and shook the crumbs from her lap.

'I'll come with you,' Elkie said, 'I've a letter I must write.' She said it distractedly as she stared at the roses and the melting curls of butter on the pale yellow plate.

Mme Smekens folded her newspaper; Elkie pressed firmly on the writing pad,

Dear Ivan,

I know it's awfully soon to be writing, but you left so suddenly yesterday, without any warning, that we didn't have much time to talk. I'm sorry I got so drunk. I hope you have a successful business trip. I'm on my way back to London now (as you can see the writing is rather shaky!).

Of course, it's too soon to have heard from you, but I'm

hoping for a letter shortly. Please tell me, how are you? Do excuse the red ink, my blue biro faded out.

Oh Ivan, I have so many memories now that I will always have! Do you know that I had never seen the sea before? Not ever. I didn't tell you the first time we went to the beach. The sea will always be for me like it was that first time, so cold and blue and frightening. I kept all those shells we picked up in Etretat, the yellow ones that look like butterflies, and the grey ones, and the white ones that look like old men's toenails. They're all in my bag. I've never eaten so many exotic foods in my life, and I'm grateful you didn't tell me what the frogs' legs were till later!

I'm travelling with a Dutch lady who's so ugly you'd think she was a witch. I just hope I can find someone who speaks English when I get to Paris. The Dutch lady speaks good English. I'm sure she can tell me where to catch my train if I can't find anyone else.

Before I left I bought a little book to teach myself French. I've started studying it, but the irregular verbs are so hard, and the funny way the sentences are put together! The next time we go to France I'll understand the language a bit better, and won't feel so strange. *Il fait un temps de chien.* I said it to the Dutch lady this morning at breakfast, and she seemed rather impressed.

She never gets off the train when we stop at stations because she thinks bandits will cut her fingers off. Isn't that funny? She has two rings, a sapphire and a ruby, and she takes them off at night and puts them in a drawstring bag inside her slip. She snores too. Do I snore, Ivan?

The weather's getting cooler the farther north we go. How's the weather where you are? Do you want to know something? You know when you got on that train yesterday morning, I had this funny feeling that I'd never see you again. Wasn't that silly of me? I guess it was because I was so drunk.

I should stop now. You've probably had enough of my shaky writing anyway. Think of me, Ivan, won't you? And write. Please write.

Elkie took an envelope and laid it across the writing pad, then scored out her parents' address. She saw the widow reading her paper, moving from side to side with the motion of the train. The fringe on the bottom of the window shade was dancing.

She finished the last of the wine watching herself cry in the mirror above Mme Smekens's head. It was so civilized: the crimson upholstery, the shiny brass plates, the varnished wood. She stared in disbelief at the envelope. She didn't know his address. He had never given her one.

The station was open at one end, the glass roof supported by black lace ironwork. Elkie looked up, not wanting Mme Smekens to see her red face.

Mme Smekens waved for a porter. A small man with frizzy hair pulled a trolley towards them. The porter loaded the widow's cases. Her jewels were back in place, the large, cut stones shining in the morning light. The porter made a comment about her rings, and she quickly pulled on her gloves.

'Where are we?' Elkie asked her, still staring at the roof.

'Why we're in Paris, of course.' The widow was agitated. The porter was staring at her gloved hands.

'I mean,' she said, 'which station are we at?'

'The *Gare St-Lazare*. Can't you read?'

'I have to get to the *Gare du Nord*. Do you know the Metro—'

'And I must get back to Amsterdam. My plants must be half-dead.' The nervous widow, escorted by her porter, sailed past. A wheel of her trolley caught Elkie's suitcase and it fell open. They didn't stop. She watched them until they were at the gate at the end of the platform. They melted into the crowd.

She knelt to push the clothes back and saw her reflection in the mirror. Her mother had bought it on her honeymoon and glued it, for richer or poorer, to the new sateen-lined lid.

Elkie picked up her bag and walked carefully down the middle of the platform. Near the door was a flower seller. The Dutch widow had said the ancient Egyptians wore yellow as their colour of mourning. '*Une rose*,' she said in her halting, phrase-book French. '*Je voudrais . . . je voudrais une jaune rose*.'

15

And now, look, she has left, . . .
And the man looks round:
in the moment of her departure
she turned everything upside down
out of the drawers of the chest.
Boris Pasternak, 'Parting'

From the door of the London restaurant he watched her; the profusity of potted palms hid him from her view. Helen Doran was wearing a long-sleeved black dress, a black beret and Italian high-heeled shoes that matched the colour of her mouth.

He saw her self-consciously shape her lips in the compact mirror, her generous mouth slightly open. In the half-hour she'd waited for him, she'd eaten most of the incarnadine redness off her lips.

He was late, late enough to see that she was concerned about the impression she'd make, and so he waited until she'd darkened her lips, smoothed her hair, three times changed her mind about the best position for her Japanese ivory pin. He remained hidden for a moment longer so she wouldn't think she had been observed, and then walked over to their table.

'Helen,' he said, 'you look absolutely marvellous in a beret.'

'Do I?' she said, as though she did not quite believe him. 'I've never had the courage to wear one before.' He leaned down and she kissed him firmly on both cheeks. 'I do wish you'd been on time,' she said. 'People will think I'm dining with a poorly paid gigolo.'

He smiled. 'You never change, do you?'

'And you look more like James every year. I was so nervous waiting that I thought I'd treat myself to an absinthe. I pretended that I was meeting him. Wasn't that silly of me? It was silly of me to do that after all these years. Still you are the next best thing to James, aren't you?'

That tight smile, the one he'd seen in the mirror. But it wasn't just that; the Pernod he'd seen her drink too quickly had made her slightly drunk, slightly uncontrolled like her thick, Botticelli hair.

'You must tell me about your trip to France,' she said. 'Thank you for your card, by the way. It brought back quite a few memories. Did you have a good time?'

'It was a bit of a disaster, I'm afraid.'

'Oh?'

'Would you like one of these?'

She stared in disbelief at the turquoise-blue cigarette he offered her; she hesitated before finally taking it. 'I didn't know you smoked these.'

'Luz bought them for me.'

'So you're still with her. I thought you'd have tired of *her* months ago.' He did not miss the delicate contempt with which she coloured the word.

'Why do you say that?'

'Because you're a hedonist. You like change.'

'You're being very hard on me,' he said, pretending to study the padded menu she'd asked for in his absence. 'Have you decided what you want?'

'I'll let you order,' she said. 'It's wonderful to have a man again to order dinner.'

'How about oysters?' he asked. 'I know how much you love them. The first Ostend ones of the season are in.'

The waiter hurried in with a platter of molluscs. They were large, plump and creamy. They quivered in their shells.

'You know,' he said picking up his oyster fork, 'whenever I eat these now I think of Chekhov.'

'Whatever for?'

'Because of a book I read. Chekhov died in Germany at some resort where he'd gone to have his lungs treated. They sent his body back to Russia in a railway car that had "For Oysters" painted on the sides.'

Because of her nerves and the alcohol, Helen started to giggle; she put her hand quickly over her mouth. 'I am sorry,' she apologized, 'but it is terribly funny.'

'Well,' he said, 'Gorky didn't think so. He was furious that Russia's great man of letters was brought home in a refrigerated oyster car. After the funeral, he wrote his wife a letter saying how disgusted he was with the crowd's behaviour. According to his account, they spent more time ogling him and Chaliapin than mourning Chekhov. And the final vulgarity, the one that Gorky couldn't excuse, was the Cossack widow that Chekhov was buried next to, one Olga Kukaretkina.'

'What did he have against the poor woman?'

'Well, loosely translated, Kukaretkina means something like "cock-a-doodle-doo carriage". The poor bugger didn't have a sense of humour. If Chekhov had been around to appreciate it, I think he would have been rather amused.'

Ivan stared for a moment at the pristine whiteness of the tablecloth, and then began to attack the shellfish with his fork. Helen unfolded her napkin and laid it carefully across her lap. For some reason, the sight of him devouring the oysters like that offended her. She felt at that moment like they looked: plump, vulnerable, quivering.

'So Helen,' he said, 'how are you? You're looking magnificent.'

'Am I?' She picked up her dessertspoon like a hand mirror and smiled into the bowl. 'If I didn't know you better, Ivan, I might just believe you. I've put on a stone since last autumn. So I look magnificent, do I? James was like that, a great one for the flattery. He knew it turned my head.'

'Do start,' Ivan said, indicating the platter, 'before I eat them all.'

They continued to eat their seafood in silence, neither of them referring to why they were there. Coward, he swallowed his mother's cold word with each oyster, coward, another

Ostend oyster sliding down, coward, that word his mother had used on his last trip home, one he'd never heard her use in reference to his father before.

Why didn't she speak? He felt it was Helen's duty to speak first; he had fulfilled his part of the agreement, but she sat there, eating and drinking champagne, saying nothing.

Finally he lifted the diary he'd propped against the leg of his chair. 'Helen,' he said, sick of the silence and the word sliding down his throat, and the briny taste of the oysters.

'What is it that you want to know?' she said. 'It won't change anything.'

He laid the book on the table between them. 'Everyone deserves to know the truth, Helen, sooner or later.'

'Do they?' she said. 'The truth isn't everyone's prerogative.'

'The truth gives you dignity,' he said. 'Besides, that was the arrangement. The diary—'

'For what I know. You always were good at bargaining.' She smiled and covered her crêpe-like neck with her fingers. 'Remember when we'd go sculling in Loch Foyle for lobsters? How much did you make that woman pay you? Wasn't it four shillings a pound? You were quite a businessman, even then.'

He pushed the book across the cloth towards her. 'No,' she said. 'Keep it. Keep it until you're satisfied with this truth of yours.'

She lifted her champagne glass. 'Cheers,' she said, then tipped it all back. 'You do surprise me, you know, saying that you still see her. She's nothing but a little savage. A little doll to undress until the next one comes along—'

'Maybe in the beginning,' he interrupted, 'but she's no more a doll than you were.' In anger he pushed his platter of empty shells away; they clattered against the inner rim of the dish.

'I'm going to marry her,' he said. He wanted to see her tipsy reaction to the falsehood flash across her face. 'I'm going to marry her,' he repeated. 'Here,' he said, handing her the engagement notice, 'read this if you don't believe me.'

'I'm sorry,' she blurted out. 'I didn't mean to offend you.

How was I to know she was different? You never tell me anything any more.'

He stared at Helen for a moment, remembering his tangled shirts in Cabourg, the clothes Luz had thrown all over the floor. The unpaired shower of socks had been her protestation, the way she had voiced her despair. 'I don't want to talk about that now,' he said, lighting another turquoise cigarette. 'That's not why we're here.'

'No,' she said, 'I guess not. All right, Ivan, if you think it's what you really want. I can't give you the answers. I can only tell you what happened.'

Her low voice droned on over the platters of fresh seafood. '. . . that Christmas Eve James fought with your mother about the divorce. I could hear them shouting downstairs. After an hour or so, James came up and told me to pack my things. He was in the strangest mood. Almost euphoric. He wouldn't tell me what Sarah had said, just that he had a plan that he didn't want to discuss. We went out to the greenhouse and got drunk. Horribly drunk to celebrate.' She laughed. 'Sarah never found us in the greenhouse. She always managed to find us everywhere else. Funny, but that's what I remember most about that night, James being so happy and so drunk. Then around four that afternoon the paraffin in the heater ran out, and then he kissed me and said I'd see him in the morning. The next thing I knew, he was dead.'

'Then you weren't with him in the boat—'

'There was no boat,' she said. 'That was something your mother invented. The greenhouse was the last time I saw him alive.'

It was the last time he had seen him, too. He found them together that day in the greenhouse. He'd seen some shadows from his room and had gone down to explore. It was dusk; they did not see him; they were naked, lying near the door. He'd seen them like that in Cabourg: the boy's clear memory of her clothes, the cream umbrella with flounces and mother-of-pearl handle lying on the terrazzo floor.

And then, a few hours later, his mother told him his father was dead. He did not believe her. He and Helen went rowing, she said, and their boat overturned and they drowned. And he did not believe her. He'd heard them in the greenhouse; he'd heard them talk of going away. He'd seen Helen leaving with her bags.

They'd gone away together and would come back one evening, his father's pockets full of the gifts that he'd been promised: with Czech eggs you could look into, or the painted barrels nested inside each other, each barrel smaller than the one before, and in the last barrel a cat with its head poking out. He wasn't dead, but on a trip somewhere with Helen, and they would return one night as they always did, smiling in the hallway, smelling of cigar smoke and Helen's distinctive French perfume.

'When James had been found, your mother came to me and paid me to go. She paid me handsomely to keep my mouth shut about what had happened and to go. I would have gone anyway, but I took her money. I would have been stupid not to. She didn't want a scandal. She was determined James's suicide should be kept a secret from you. She even bought off the coroner. Aren't you grateful? It's amazing the things money can do.'

She looked at him. 'Is that enough?' she said. 'Have you had your pound of flesh? Good,' she said, picking up the diary. 'After all these years we both have what we want and it doesn't change a bloody thing.'

Coward, that word again pressing to the front of his mouth. 'Where did she find him?'

'At the avenue of trees,' she said, 'lying in four inches of dirty water. *Slàinte,* Ivan,' she said, picking up her glass again, '*slàinte*.'

16

A touch of the old trouble

Stevie Smith, 'Emily Writes Such a Good Letter'

'You all right?' The woman leaned across the park bench. She wore Indian bracelets and a red dress, and had heavy gold loops hanging from her ears. 'You been here for hours. I seen you when I go to work this mornin' an' you still here. You all right?' She moved her hands as she spoke, and the thin, metal bracelets jingled against each other like chimes.

'Leave me alone.'

'Now you go along home now. This park ain't nowhere to be at night.'

'I told you to leave me alone.' The girl continued to stare into her lap.

'Look here, girl. You wet as a dog an' sittin' there! Now you go home, or I takes you along with me.'

She smoothed the damp skirt clinging to her thighs. 'I told you I don't want to go home.'

The woman poured the dregs of the girl's wine into the grass and pulled her, gently, to her feet. 'Ain't nothing here 'cept some ol' coots an' they can't fly right. You comin' along with me. I'm not leavin' you here. I can't sleep tonight if I do.'

The girl followed her in silence along the arc-shaped lake. She counted the empty deck chairs, the colour of red-white ribbon candy, as precisely, as ineffectually as she counted the slippage of days since he had been gone.

The woman turned to see if she was still being followed.

'What your name, girl?'

'Luz.'

'Loose. That a mighty strange name. Loose. You a loose woman?' The woman began to laugh. 'I'm Malverna. Look like you carryin' a whole pocketful of trouble with you.'

They had reached the boundary of the park and Elkie turned to go. Malverna said, 'Now you come this far, you welcome to come an' sit in front of the fire. You don't look like you in any kind of hurry anyway. There a few more things I need to buy for supper. You want to come pickin' an' pullin' with me?'

At the street market Malverna waddled from cart to cart picking up tomatoes, pinching pullet breasts, shaking coconuts, shaking her finger. 'No milk in this copra an' you tryin' to sell it, man! Been on the tree too long. Dry as an ol' woman's teat. An' a pound of lady fingers, bandit, an' make it weigh right.'

The flat where she lived had no gate, only two posts. The door was painted a flamboyant pink. She led the girl into the front room and stood her in front of the gas fire. 'I'll be with you in one minute. Malverna's got to go to the loo.'

On one side of the fireplace was a picture of the Virgin Mary and underneath, a small shelf with bright, plastic flowers. On the other side was the map of an island. Across the mantelpiece were wedding photographs. In all of them the grooms looked stiff and awkward, their faces coal-dark above their snow-white collars.

'So glad you want a long engagement, so send us a picture of him and yourself and bring him home at Christmas,' and after that damn letter mammy went and put an announcement in the paper! God, how could they do it to me? If Ivan ever found out that 'Mr and Mrs Francis Bonner of Dungiven are pleased to announce the engagement of their daughter, Miss Ethel Louise Bonner to—' Jesus he would kill me.

Thank goodness my gran sent it on to me or I'd never have known. I can never lift my head again in the town because everyone will think I've been jilted. I can just hear me da in the shop, 'Haven't you heard the latest? Our Elkie's been jilted by her fancy man from Pellipar.'

Malverna returned and pulled the curtains closed. She picked up a tin on the side-table and prised open the lid. 'Snuff?' Malverna giggled at the expression on the girl's face. 'No,' she said, 'of course not. Snuff is for ol' women who don't care what they smells like. Come along with me now an' get out of them wet clothes.'

She took her into the bedroom. Above the bed a small oil lamp burned beneath another picture of the Virgin. 'Come on, off with them. Don't be shy. Malverna seen more naked women than the Queen of England. Everything off. Everything. A body nothing to be ashame of.'

She took the girl's wet clothes and draped them over a clotheshorse at the foot of the bed. Half-naked, Elkie was staring at her dolls. Propped against the ruffled, orange pillows was a row of dolls with milk-white faces, starched dresses and pouting, crooked mouths.

Malverna threw her a dressing gown. 'Here, you wrap this aroun' yourself. You like my dolls?' She put her hand on the curly, blonde wig nearest her. 'This my first. I name her Weekswages. Winston buy for me. That what she cost. She belong to an ol' Creole woman who dead an' all her estate things get auctioned. An' this Matilda, Katharine, Juliet, Anna.' She touched each one on the head.

When I got back his stains were still there, halfway down the sheet. I saw shapes in them: islands and clouds and lakes. After he'd gone, I never wanted to wash those sheets, never. I lay with the bedclothes pulled back and pressed my nose against the clouds, and his smell was still there.

When Malverna turned back to the girl she was crying. 'Now, now. Sit yourself down here in front of the fire an' tell Malverna why you sits on a park bench the whole day long. This man trouble?'

She buried her face in her arms. 'I can't understand it. I just can't understand it.'

Malverna knelt in front of her. She spoke softly. 'When a girl, all young an' pretty, look like you,' she circled her hands in the air, 'hair an' face all whichway, I jus' know it got to be a man. Ol' Malverna,' she said, 'she know a thing or two. I cry my eyes out too once upon a time.'

Malverna pushed the wad of tobacco to one side of her cheek. 'My Winston, before we come here, was a farm worker in Dominique, an' he move from fiel' to fiel' with the crop. He take up with some girl in each village an' make baby with her, an' there more of his bastards from Roseau to Loubiet than chickens—'

'Flash was a gigolo,' he'd said. 'He'd wander as far as Ballykelly to deposit his seed in another dancing, young bitch. I say to each lady I bed, no pups till we're wed. His master,' he'd said, 'is infinitely more discriminating.'

'. . . an' me, I can't make baby an' it break my heart, it jus' about break my heart. I stay at home an' cry an' cry till Mammy Sylvester say to me, "Now you sits here, Malverna, an' cry till Mr Gabriel blow on his mighty horn, an' it won't do you no good. Winston come back to you, don't he? He give you money an' he care for you, don't he? Why no woman could want more! My ol' man he sits at home, don't work, steal my money to buy rum to drink till he pie-eyed. We don't got nothing but a roof over our head, an' even that damn roof leak. Look aroun' at what you got, Malverna. A mail-order bed an' chairs an' a table. Now dry your eyes an' thank the good Lord for what you got."

'Yes sir, that what she say to me, an' I remember. I remember the good sense she talk into me. Yes sir. She make me see that my Winston is a good man—'

He's a good man, the best I know. It's just that he's never felt this way before and it frightens him. Even that first night I frightened him. He thought I was a Catholic because of the gold cross I wore around my neck. But I told him I wasn't a Catholic, and that I didn't plan to be a nun either. But I won't stay a nun for him. I've been a nun for too long. So I sit in my chair and burn candles, and I pretend. I pretend that any moment he'll throw a stone against my window; I pretend that my finger belongs to him.

I'll never forget the night I put the kettle on for some tea, and then we went to bed and forgot about it. The kettle boiled and boiled and steamed up the windows, and after he'd come out of me, I happened to look over and all the things I'd written on the window showed through the steam: IVAN + LUZ. POOKIE, I LOVE YOU SO. OH WHAT A LOVELY COCK YOU HAVE. FUCK ME. STAY INSIDE ME FOREVER. *I swear I could have died. 'Oh,' I said real casual-like, 'I lost my earring in the sheets, Ivan. Will you try and find it for me? I've got to turn the kettle off before it boils dry.' And all the time I had the earring in my hand. I got up to rub out that steamy letter so's it wouldn't frighten him. And I did rub it out. I rubbed it all out except one word. Just one word. STAY.*

'. . . an' he work hard to buy us passage here. It was the thing in Dominique, you know, everyone goin' over, an' the ones left behind would never leave the island. We thought that everybody in England was rich.' She giggled. 'We did. Everyone was goin' to England then. You heard so much about England at school, an' me an' Winston thought we goin' to England to where the streets is paved with gold.'

Malverna took Elkie's hand. 'Well,' she said, 'that enough talkin' in here. I got to get that cookin' started. I takes you to the kitchen, an' tell you the story of how we come to England on a ship called the *Francasea*.'

Elkie scanned the small kitchen, stared at the fish heads in wax paper by the sink. *Teach me to swim, little fish. Teach me to swim, Ivan, or I'll drown. I'll drown if you don't hold me up out of the ice-white bath.*

'. . . it was small, not like the big ones. It was the *Francasea*'s last voyage an' I tell you, we had some trouble on there. We had engine trouble for two days an' nights in the middle of the ocean. No land. No land, jus' sea an' sky.' Malverna was slicing lady's fingers. The viscous, green wheels spun as they dropped into the bowl.

'An' we done well here. We rents our own place an' lives our own lives an' don't have to share a room with no one. An' now I save to go back one day. An' the first meal I want to sit down to there is mountain chicken. Traditional dish of Dominique. It a delicacy. Very expensive. Only Americans can afford it any more. It that way because the men have to go out an' climb the mountains, high up after a rain, because mountain chicken only come out after a rain. You know what mountain chicken is, Loose? Is a frog! Heh, heh, frog!'

I've never eaten so many exotic foods in my life, and I'm glad you didn't tell me what the frogs' legs were till later. You want to know something, Ivan? Something I didn't tell you in the letter. After you got on the train that morning I felt like I was gonna spew. I had to go to the bog and squat on those big shoes coming out of the porcelain and I passed out. I came to in the basin and my clothes were all wet and Jesus, you can't imagine what I smelled like.

'. . . but that will be my first meal, mountain chicken. I want to die in Dominique with a drumstick in my mouth, an' the sunshine on my face, an' I'll be a happy woman, yes sir, yes sir!' Malverna pointed to the sink. 'You do me a favour, Loose, and throw them heads in that big pot.'

Elkie walked to the basin. The silvery eyes focused on the ceiling. The heads had been chopped off just beneath the gills. 'Yes sir,' she said, 'we havin' fish broth tonight. We good Catholics here!'

He had fish that night. I remember. A dead eye stared at me from the sauce. 'You hate fish,' she heard herself saying.

'What you talkin' about, girl? I not hate fish. Malverna like fish.'

Elkie lifted the iron pot off the stove and set it near the sink. Closing her eyes, she lifted the paper by the edges and slid the heads in. 'Now you jus' pour some water, jus' enough to cover them, and put them back on the stove. Yes, nice fish broth tonight with sulphur dasheen, ladyfingers and pigeon peas.'

The kitchen was humid from the steaming pots. Malverna took off her blouse and hung it on the back of her chair. 'Whew!' she said, 'that much better. Ol' Malverna sweat a lot, an' it good to get home an' get comfortable.' She picked up another dasheen and began to peel it. 'Tonight I put on my lilac dress an' go to Mass. I feel like a carnival queen in that dress! I spray Jungle Gardenia on my neck, an' I feel like a young girl back in Dominique. Now you stayin' for supper with me an' Winston?'

'Thank you. You've been wild kind, but I'm not much company now. I'd best be going along home.'

'Why you know you welcome to stay an' eat. You need some eatin' by the looks of you. Like a rag doll lost her stuffin'.' Her breasts shook as she beat a thick batter. 'I believe in eatin'. I say if you have twopence, put it inside your stomach an' then it's yours. Nobody can take it away. Now this coconut bread is one of Malverna's specialities. Ain't nobody who's eaten it not come back wantin' more.'

Wanting him, wanting him outside my window. The bell was out of order when I moved into Mrs Ducker's. On the fourth evening that I was there, I heard something at the window. I looked out and he was bending down at the kerb, trying to find another stone. He looked up at me, grinned, and threw it straight up in the air.

'Want a drop of rum? Winston has nice Jamaica rum his brother send him for Christmas.' Malverna opened a cupboard above the sink and brought out a bottle and three glasses, and filled each to the brim. 'Winston be home soon.'

Elkie stared at the stitched cups of the white brassière resting on Malverna's chest. *Your da and I do not see why you do not come home now or say at Christmas at the latest. We have tried to be patient since you've been living in the Big Smoke, but now we feel you should come home for a visit and bring your fiancé with you so's we can settle on a date for the wedding—*

'You drink that right down. It warm you up, make you feel better.' She tapped her watch-glass. 'That Winston still not here. He must be out dancin' again with some *labasse* woman.'

'Your husband's out dancing with a woman?'

Malverna giggled. 'Why that man got them lined up aroun' Cadiz Road.' She lifted the wrist bangled with thin bracelets.

'Hear that? I tease Winston that so he can hear Malverna comin'. I tell you, one day I come home from the hospital early an' I foun' Winston in my bed with a woman, naked as the day they was born.'

'Jesus, what'd you do?'

'I said, "Get that thing goin' again. Malverna show you how it done right." '

'But how can you live with someone that's done that to you?'

'It the devil you know, or it the devil you don't. I know my devil and I love him. I do.'

'What's he like?'

'What my Winston like? We is like day an' night. He Jack Spratt, eat no fat. We meet at a dance in Loubiet, Winston an' me. I be sixteen an' the way that man move, why it turn my knees to guava jelly. He move like so, an' the priest come up between us an' separate us an' start shoutin' "Satan is at work here, Satan is at work!" An' Winston, he jus' laugh an' laugh, an' whisper in my ear that priests wear them robes to hide their stickin'-up all the time privates! That my Winston! Here, you drink his rum. He out with some *labasse* woman.'

Malverna refilled her own and they touched glasses. 'Loose, it sure good to have you here to talk to. Is terrible thing to eat alone. My philosophy is, so Winston sniff at some other woman's leg, he come back to me. He sleep with me. They say there ain't nothing sure in this life but death an' taxes, but Loose, I tell you, there is a love between two people that don't go away, no matter what happen, no matter how long they apart.'

Malverna wiggled her dress down in front of the mirror. 'Damn thing have side zip,' she grumbled. 'Some fool man design this dress with side zip. No man wear no clothes with fool side zip.'

'Let's try again,' Elkie said. 'Hold your breath this time. I'll count to three and then pull. Ready? One, two, three . . . got it!'

'Whew! Well, that stay up as long as I not breathe.' Malverna admired her reflection. 'Don't let them tell you nothing different, Loose. A man like meat. Like to get hold of somethin'. Not like these mosquito women, nothin' up front, nothin' behind. Man like to get his hands aroun' somethin'.'

Elkie pictured her waddling up the aisle for Mass, her ample buttocks swaying, the lilac fabric strained uncomfortably over her hips.

Malverna leaned cautiously over the vanity. 'Now where my Jesus fan?'

They walked slowly down the High Street. Malverna was wearing the carnival dress and a large, straw hat with purple flowers. 'When I little girl,' she said, 'I jus' love Sundays. I like to go get dress up. Nice hats. Panamas or nice straw hats, nice white hats, you know, an' your shoes an' socks. It nice because that the day of the week when you really dress up. You go to church, then you come home, an' then you got Sunday school in the afternoon, you go for a nice long walk or you visit. We had this woman to visit. She had this estate not far from the church, an' she had no children, an' we use to go there. She had a piano an' we use to play the piano there.'

They passed a picture framing shop with the sign, FISH TANKS MADE TO ORDER. Elkie stopped and pressed her nose against the glass. 'You know,' she said, 'all me life I've wanted a fish tank.'

'Fish tank, hell! What you need, girl, is a party. Lots to eat an' rum an' beer. We got a West Indian party on tomorrow night in Notting Hill. You come if you got nothing better to do. Outside the dance hall you find men fryin' up fish an' they makes somethin' we calls the bakes, an' roasted peanuts you get nice and hot, like in Dominique. I takes you with me, Loose, an' we stay up all night wearin' out our shoes!'

Elkie continued to stare into the window which, in its thickness and colour and shape, was like a fish tank. With the substantial woman beside her, she suddenly felt for the first time in months that she was no longer floating. 'Malverna,' she said, turning sharply around, 'there's something I want to tell you. My name isn't Luz. It's a stupid magazine name I use when I want to be someone else. My real name's Ethel, but my friends call me Elkie.'

'Never met such a girl with as many names as the Litany.' She started to laugh. 'So I call you Elkie. That right? This last name this ol' woman have to learn?'

'Yes.'

'Well,' she said, 'its good to see you smile.'

Rows of burning candles cast shadows on the statues of saints. Their thin, ravaged faces frightened her. Not the smiling Presbyterian Jesus handing out the loaves and the fishes.

A large, plaster crucifix hung above the altar. Blood dripped beneath the crown of thorns. She missed the sense of stillness, the stained-glass windows telling the story of the fisher of men.

'Malverna,' she whispered, 'why do you come here?'

'Why do I come here? I come here 'cause it give me peace.' She thumped the middle of her chest with her fist. 'It give me peace right here.'

As she walked up the aisle Malverna nodded to several women; they all wore hats and gloves and bright dresses. Malverna genuflected in front of the altar and then they sat in the first pew.

'What's that strange smell?'

'That incense, Elkie. Ain't you never been inside a Catholic church before?' The woman heaved herself off the pew and knelt on the low railing, her fingers entwined with purple beads. She heard her mumbling, 'Hail Mary, full of grace—'

I sit and pray he will come. He will not come. If I pin up my hair with permanent-wave clips and put fresh garlic in my soup.

Malverna sat down again. The woman sitting beside her said, 'What pretty gloves you got there! They are fine!'

'They Chartres lace. My sister foun' them in Roseau after the hurricane. All the houses been lifted off their foundation. Clothes was lyin' all over the street. She said she thought it was the end of the world 'cause it was broad daylight, an' suddenly everywhere jus' got black, an' the waves were like mountains, like mountains. She thought it was jus' comin' to cover the whole island. She got to go across the road 'cause she lost her whole roof, you know, an' she said she couldn't see for all the sand gettin' into her eyes 'cause the wind was blowin' it so hard. I tell you, when she came back she foun' a sail-fish in the middle of her bed.'

The women were laughing when the priest entered; the congregation stood up. The priest began to speak. He lifted his hands. She watched Malverna's lips moving, whispering to herself. She looked into her lap and, in the folds of her dress, she imagined she saw his face.

'Malverna,' she said, 'I think I'm gonna be sick.'

'Open your eyes, Elkie.'

'They are open. The room's spinning.'

'That jus' the rum, Elkie. That jus' the whirling pits. Hold my hand. Squeeze it tight.' She did; the French lace traced a cathedral into her palm.

The windows of the train were down. He stood at one of them in his white suit and hat and waved. 'I promise I'll write,' he said leaning out of the window, the train pulling away, 'I promise I'll write.'

'You'll be all right. Jus' you keep hold of my hand now.'

He wasn't waving any more; both his hands were on top of the glass. Elkie jerked her hand away. She ran out of the church as she had run after his train, forcing the rum to stay down until she safely reached the street.

17

I fly, I float. I walk on air. Some time later
I bolt back to sea suddenly.

Rosalind Belben, *The Limit*

He jumps from my bed. I watch him dress. To tuck in his shirt he undoes his fly. I see his cock, his fur. He watches me watch. Does he see that I love him? No.

He says, I can never show as much emotion as you. I'm afraid to. I didn't want to see you again. Something made me come back. I don't understand it. I don't know what it was.

I lie in the warmth of my bed listening to the knocking, steady at my door. I'm dreaming.

Who is it, I say, standing behind the door in my thermal underwear, hair pinned up with permanent-wave clips (I am the bride of Frankenstein), who's there? Mrs Ducker. Ducker with her pink face saying, Turn that bleedin' radio off! It's two o'clock in the morning and some people have to get up for work—

Ivan. It's Ivan.

I open the door. He smells of cigarettes and beer. I help him off with his boots. He stands, white and naked, above me. Touch me, he says, touch me, moving my hands, pushing my head lower. Closer.

I think I'm dreaming. I get up to stop the drip in the kitchen. I'm awake. The alarm rings. It's 6.30. There's light at the window. He mounts me again. He's not drunk now. He can't be.

I get up to make coffee. It runs down my leg in a little river. I deceive myself again. I'm getting better at it.

I wake at night and listen to the cars drive past my window. I cry into the pillow so I won't make so much noise. In the day I cry, too, but not into the pillow. The pillow I save for night.

I stop, lift my knee to hip level. He reaches across my body and lays his hand on my forehead. A penny for your thoughts, a penny.

I sit crying in the bathtub, steam clouding the tiles; he was asleep while I cried in my bed. Are you trying to give me a sermon? he asks and kisses my neck. I sit in the seat he has made for me with his body and disbelievingly pinch my arm.

A gypsy comes to the door with curlers in her hair and a scarf knotted beneath her chin. She leans against the door jamb and says, A charm for you, love. I'll tell your fortune. You'll be lucky. I can see it in your face. She dangles a huge, glowing shamrock in front of my eyes. You've had a bit of a setback, haven't you, love? A setback, but you've got a good man. You'll be the mother of a son. I'd love to read your fortune.

I go upstairs to get some change; I cross her palm with silver. It isn't enough. She leaves quickly, taking all her charms with her.

I dream of carrying heavy dishes and drop them, smash bottles of champagne. He says, You must tell me the story of Rumpelstiltskin. We sit reading, he on the chair, I on the bed. He removes everything except a thin, cotton shirt and parts my legs.

I am in my room, waiting. His rainy-day fuck. Tears catch in my hair. Lying on the bed he was to have been in, beating the sheets.

I pull my clothes on. They are cold against my body. My nipples tighten when they are touched. The cunt easily takes my finger, two fingers, four.

I run down a hill. I let gravity pull me, my legs not really working. I turn the corner. A slight rise, then a flat stretch, then a steep rise again before the posts that mark the edge of a heath. I run and run; I don't stop, not even to look at the lake with the ducks, the coots that don't know how to land.

Only in dreams he comes to me, his arms close to his body. He stares at the ceiling-rose, his hands folded beneath his oxters. I want to ask him, A penny—but even for a fortune he would not let me enter his head.

I never remember hearing the buzzer or going downstairs or taking the permanent-wave clips out of my hair, just the sight of him there, smiling.

I don't know why he comes, even in dreams, because after I clear the dishes away, he says he will not stay.

I bleed like a pig, a river of blood on the sheet. Don't lift the blanket, please don't! O Ivan, O my love. Don't you know I talk in my sleep? I could have told you I talk in my sleep. I talk such bloody nonsense in my sleep.

18

"You shouldn't have danced like that."
Muriel Stuart, 'In the Orchard'

Her nights were often spent like that now: half-waking, half-dreaming. He inhabited her, an incubus that disappeared at morning, a shade afraid of first light. She sat up in bed and ran her finger down the wall. In France the first thing she had seen was his freckled back.

She pulled her dressing gown around her and stumbled into the kitchen to heat some water. On the refrigerator was a stack of dirty plates, a skinned potato, the skeleton of a chicken from the week before, the mushrooms black and shrivelled against the sides of the enamel dish.

Outside it was raining. She stood by the window and looked down the hill. A man ran by under an enormous black umbrella. She watched it, bobbing, to the foot of the hill.

After the eggs had boiled, she lifted them out of the pan; she held one up to the light. Ivan's mother had blown eggs. Sarah had said when they were taking the decorated shells out of the cabinet, that it was useful to know how to blow an egg because then you could keep it forever. Elkie stared in disbelief at the two eggs rolling on her pink plate; she didn't remember making two.

When she went downstairs for the mail, there was a postcard addressed to her from Ivan; it was a picture of swans floating on a river. After reading it, she slowly climbed the stairs.

On the landing she stopped outside her door to touch the Athena poster which provided the only brightness in the otherwise dingy hall. After reading his postcard, she wanted to lift the canvas of van Gogh's covered wagon, to curl up in the red bed of that gypsy caravan, and hide.

To kill the morning she rearranged her books and then decided to clean the windows. She sponged, soaped and rinsed each pane. She dried the glass with newspaper, swinging her arm in great arcs, the words on his card taunting her: *where many things end, where many things end*. She threw the wad of soggy newsprint against the wall. Malverna had said to come over at eight tonight if she wanted to go to that party. To come to Notting Hill unless she had something better to do.

She picked up the smallest elephant on the windowsill; it was the colour of Malverna's skin. She moved the baby elephant with the swaying motion of the beast in the forest, the foliage from the dead plants speckling its tough, beautifully rough skin.

The party was on the third floor of an old building. Orange paper lanterns covered the lights. Near the door was a huge punchbowl on a table. Malverna handed their bottles of rum to a man in a ruffled shirt who presided over the punch floating with oranges, lemons and limes.

It was so dark; the only source of light in the room was a standard lamp with a sateen shade; its tasselled fringe shimmied with the dancers.

'Whew!' Malverna said. 'It hotter than hell in here. No air, no air. You know what I like right now, Elkie? A vanilla cornet. I tell you the story of the first time Winston buy me a cornet. I not know to eat the cornet because I never had one before, jus' ice cream, you see? So I eat the ice cream takin' care not to break that cornet. When I finish I wash it all clean an' hand it back to he, an' he say, "Why Malverna, you got to eat this!" That the first time I had a cornet. Oh dear!' She wiped the tears off her cheeks. 'But it not so funny at sixteen, no sir, no sir.'

'Malverna,' a man called out from the crowd, 'ain't you a

vision in your red shoes?'

She screamed, throwing her hands back, 'Why if it ain't you, Algernon! You jus' the man I been waitin' to see! I wear my Dorothy shoes jus' for you, man.' She put an arm around his waist and said, 'Algernon, I want you to meet a good friend of mine. Elkie, this is Algernon.'

When the girl put out her hand, he kissed it. 'I'm delighted,' he said. 'She's a beauty an' no cousin of yours, Malverna, so we don't have to behave ourselves.'

She slapped his hand playfully. 'You got to watch these black men, Elkie. Like centipedes. They crawl into your clothes at night an' you got to shake them out. Now Algernon an' I goin' upstairs. You be all right here. If you need anything, you jus' shout. Before we go on up, this good man get you another glass of rum.'

She took his postcard out of her pocket and smoothed its bent corner. It was a photograph of the Limmatquai in Zürich with swans feeding on the river. On the reverse side she had already memorized what it said: *Arrived here en route to Basle. Dull, quiet, cold. Reading F. Scott Fitzgerald. He was right—'Switzerland is a country where very few things begin, but many things end.'*

She smashed her thigh with her fist. When she looked up, half-crying, she saw a man across the room staring at her. She couldn't tell how old he was; his clothes confused her. He wore a red shirt open at the neck and a psychedelic cravat. Beneath his bell-bottomed trousers he had the whitest of shoes. He smiled, slightly ingenuously, as though it were a smile he had practised often in front of a mirror, like a skittish actor.

She smiled at him because she didn't know what else to do, and then he was standing beside her saying, 'Why I'll dance with you. Ain't no reason why a girl pretty as you be sittin' here by yourself.' He offered her his hand and, because she didn't know how to refuse, he took hers and pushed his way through the crowd to the middle of the room.

She felt his hand in the middle of her back, her breasts

flattened against his chest. 'You a real good dancer,' he said. 'What's your name?'

'Butter and crame.'

'Come on, tell me your name.'

'Butter and crame,' she insisted. 'Ask me again and I'll tell you the same.'

'Then I call you Butter,' he said smugly. 'You come to West Indian parties much?'

'This is my first.'

'You smell so nice,' he said. 'That expensive perfume you got on. A gift from one of your boyfriends?'

'The Aga Khan.' It was the perfume she'd worn when she'd gone to that dance on the river. In the bathroom she'd sprayed herself with a cloud of it, not believing she had been the woman she saw in the mirror, a carnation behind her ear like a Spanish dancer, her hair sleeked away from her face like a seal.

She was glad when the record ended and he said he was thirsty. 'How about you, Butter?'

She nodded. 'It's wild hot in here.'

He threw his head back and laughed. 'Well, it get a lot hotter. Why the evenin' jus' beginnin' to make you melt!'

Standing by the curtainless window, she saw the street below was deserted. It made her feel even more alone. She wondered what he was doing, who he was with. The music started again and she watched the couples dance slowly, languorously in the heat, the way they they had moved at Cabourg. "Have another cream cake," he'd said, looking up the Avenue de la Mer towards the sea.

"Why didn't you tell me sooner you'd only be here four days?"

"I didn't want to spoil your holiday."

"And you think you haven't spoiled it now? Are you trying to tell me it would have all been different if I'd had long nails and cocktail dresses? If I could have swept in and out of that bloody hotel lobby—"

Her partner nudged her elbow. 'Here's that drink. Cheers.'

'Cheers,' she said perfunctorily; there was none in her voice.

'Jus' think,' he said, 'in a few months you'll be sittin' in front of a two-bar heater wonderin' where this beautiful summer gone.'

He held her tightly against him as they moved across the floor. She brushed the naked backs of black women, their skin a strange colour beneath the orange-shaded lights.

She felt his leg slide confidently between hers; he tried to kiss her. His whiskers scraped her cheek when she quickly turned away. 'Come on,' he said, 'jus' a little kiss. Jus' a little kiss for Winston.'

'Winston?' Elkie pushed him away. 'Get away! Get away from me or I'll call the police!'

The couples nearest them had stopped dancing and were laughing. The tasselled shade still shimmied, making strange shapes on the wall. Elkie pushed her way through their laughter and ran downstairs. To her relief no one followed her.

The street light threw a coolie's hat on the pavement. She stood for a while outside the bright hat, watching the shadows of the black dancers on the floor above, then the black shapes of the moths as they flew fearlessly against the scorching globes of light.

19

At a time of such uncertain certainties
such certain uncertainties
—it's dark in this room—
Antonín Bartušek, 'Conception'

Two weeks ago I took a chair downstairs and sat behind the front door waiting for the morning mail to come. I wanted to see if there was any word from Ivan. I knew there wouldn't be, but I sat there anyway, and watched the shadows of the people from the street pass by.

After the post came at ten, I picked through it three or four times. There was only one thing addressed to me, a circular headed, WE PREACH CHRIST IN ALL THE SCRIPTURES. Some Good Samaritan must've thought the message could resurrect me.

About noon Mrs Ducker came in from shopping. I still hadn't found the energy to get myself back up the stairs. She nearly screamed when she saw me sitting behind the door. 'What are you doing here?' she asked, her face even more flushed than usual. I told her I was waiting for my ship to come in.

'Well you frightened the life out of me,' she said, cupping her breast. The next thing I knew I was on Mrs Ducker's couch, and a strange man was standing over me.

'You'll be all right,' he said, 'just take a sip of this.' He handed me some water. 'Have you fainted recently?' I told him that I had, in a smelly, French railway loo.

'How long ago was that?' He scribbled something on a pad. He looked at his pocket diary and motioned for Mrs Ducker to leave the room.

When he told me, I smiled. He must have thought I was a loon. All I could see in my mind's eye were those blue-and-orange signs, BUVEZ ORANGINA, that Ivan and I had sat under on our holiday. It was as if the beverage was a panacea, as if drinking it would nullify what he'd just said. When the doctor left, I dragged myself upstairs and pulled the bedclothes over my head, and cried myself to sleep.

Every day after that got hotter and hotter. The weather office reported that it was the hottest August in seventy-six years. It's funny then how cold I felt, as though I was quite dead.

Every morning I wake up feeling dead. The days pass from one to another with little to distinguish between them. Today's Saturday; I only know that because I had to pay the milkman. The sight of all those full, white bottles on his milk float made me want to spew.

Malverna was sweeping the pavement in front of her house when I went to see her, a red scarf tied in two peaks around her head. 'Why Elkie,' she said, 'look like you carryin' a whole pocketful of trouble with you.'

When I told her, she kept shaking her head. I'd never seen her look so serious. 'In Dominique we use to do this,' and she whispered in my ear, 'but you need *obeah* for that. Ain't no *obeah* woman here.'

In the front room Malverna cooled herself with a Jesus fan; Christ strolled in the Garden of Gethsemane above thick, black letters that said,

T. SPRATT & SONS FUNERAL HOME
FUNERALS ARRANGED FOR TOWN, COUNTRY & ABROAD
WEDDING CARS FOR HIRE

She laid the fan down, Jesus side up across her thighs, and looked me straight in the eye. 'You happy 'bout this, Elkie?' She moved her fat hands in an arc over her stomach. 'You please with yourself?'

I started to cry. 'Now, now. You sits here an' cry till Mr

Gabriel blow on his big horn, an' it won't do you no good. No good at all. You jus' leave things with Malverna an' she see what she can do. She make some discreet inquiries, but she don't promise nothing. I jus' hope you knows what you want. 'Cause once you makes up your mind there ain't no goin' back. No goin' back, you hear? This wrong,' she said, 'all wrong, an' Malverna should have no part in it.'

I didn't hear from Malverna for a week. I began to think that even if she did find someone, I couldn't go through with it. Then another postcard came. Though he didn't come right out and say it, I knew he was trying to tell me he was never coming back. He was still in Switzerland eating fondue, still reading F. Scott Fitzgerald: *This is by way of explanation,* he wrote, *Fitzgerald can say it so much better than I can. 'Love is fragile— . . . —but perhaps the pieces are saved, the things that hovered on lips, that might have been said. The new love-words, the tenderness learned, and treasured up for the next lover.' I hope you can understand, Luz, what I am trying to say: that I never wanted to hurt you and that it is better like this. I also want you to know that I will miss you, and that I will never, never forget you. I wish you all the best for the future and much happiness.*

I kept reading that card, wishing Loreen was here. Mrs Ducker said while I'd been in France she'd done a moonlight flit, and disappeared with Mr Ducker's army surplus blankets. I was trying to remember what Loreen had said.

She had said she was in trouble once, and tried what a friend of hers suggested: 'the hottest bath you could stand and a whole bottle of sloe gin.' At least that's what I hoped Loreen had said, because whatever the remedy was, she said it'd done the trick handsome.

I went up to the bath during the day when everyone was at work. I hid the bottle underneath my bathrobe just in case anyone should see me. I fed the meter well and slid the bolt across the door.

The water scalded my legs. I had already unscrewed the

bottle of gin and put it behind the taps. I stared at the blue-black berries on the label, and thought about the conversation I'd once heard mammy have with Mrs Donaughey from down the road. They were in the scullery and didn't know I was standing outside the door. Mrs Donaughey said what a blessing that it had happened of its own accord, that it must have been the will of God because the last wean had nearly killed her. Ten pounds, and she'd had to have stitches and they hadn't healed properly, and that she'd been in agony for months after, and if that had been the first baby, it would have been the last, encyclical or no encyclical.

I could feel the gin: I saw four spigots and bouquets of berries. I thought of that first meeting at the avenue at Pellipar . . .

The bottle was three-quarters gone. I looked into the water, then added more hot. The bloody water was as clear as the gin.

A day later my bell rang. 'Ivan!' I screamed, 'Ivan!' Flying down the stairs two at a time, it's a wonder I didn't break my neck. It had to be him; no one else had ever come to visit.

But when I opened the front door it was Malverna. She looked terrified. 'Quick, quick, girl, don't leave me standin' out here.

'So this where you lives,' she said looking around the crowded room that Ivan had found so suffocating. 'Look,' she said, 'you know what I come about. We don't got much time. How many weeks now? So we don't got much time. I found a good woman. You come to this address tomorrow week at half past nine. Don't eat or drink nothing after six o'clock the night before. Don't you forget, Elkie. She said was real important.'

I took her hands in mine and pressed them to my face. 'Oh Malverna! I don't know how I can thank you. You've saved my life.'

She started to wail. 'Oh Elkie, this so wrong, so wrong an' Malverna don't want no part of it. These things is dangerous, but you say it what you want. It ain't for Malverna to judge what right an' what wrong. Only God can do that. Only God can do that.'

She saw a picture of Ivan by the bed. 'This him! Where this no-account man when you need him—'

'Don't say that, Malverna. He doesn't know. He doesn't know anything about it.'

'Ooo, he handsome devil, he is,' she said. 'That why you give in.'

It was my favourite photograph of him; he was wearing a black velvet Nehru jacket and a ruffled shirt. 'He look like a real lady-killer, all right. He the kind of man crawl under your skin like a jigger, make you scratch bad. Winston like that too when he young. So where this no-account man?'

'He's in Switzerland ending something.'

'Switzerland.' She screwed up her face. 'He know 'bout this. This why he left Miss Elkie.'

'No,' she said. 'He left because he didn't love me. It wasn't for any other reason.'

'Well, if that what you want to believe, Elkie, then you believe. We all got to hang onto our own raft in this sea of life. I got to go to the hospital now. Remember, nothing to eat or drink after six the night before. I'll be there to hold my Elkie's hand.'

The house was painted baby-pink. On the wall next to the door was a sign, HATTIE DANIELS—SEAMSTRESS EXTRAORDINAIRE.

After I pressed the buzzer I was surprised to see Malverna open the door. 'Come in,' she said nervously, 'come in quick, quick.'

Playing solitaire at a table in the corner was a small woman with white hair. She stood up slowly and offered me her hand. It was like a bird's claw, almost fleshless. 'First there is the matter of money,' she said. I handed her an envelope. She counted the notes twice.

The money was from mammy and Ivan, money to go home. I'd finally found the courage to write and say that he'd broken off the engagement, that Ivan didn't feel he was ready yet for the commitment of marriage, and she had written back, *If he wants to wait until he's in his late thirties to marry, Elkie, I wouldn't bother with him. He seems to cherish his freedom, and men like that are certainly no good when they do get married as they have all these habits no one can change, and they don't make good mates, only good bachelors. A tiny bit of good news. Austins have agreed to take back the orange-blossom dress, but I was too hasty with the strap shoes. I'd already dyed them.* I remembered how the money had fallen out of her letter when I'd opened it. Now it was lying all over Hattie's bed.

I thought about that as I climbed onto the cold, metal table. I thought of his face, his thin lips, the green-sea colour of his eyes. I put my feet into the stirrups, spreading my legs to Hattie Daniels the way I used to do for Ivan when the two of us were naked. When the two of us were naked and silent and, separately, alone.

20

Come now, drift up the dark, come up the drifting
sea-dark street now in the dark night seesawing like the sea,
Dylan Thomas, *Under Milk Wood*

Elkie put up her umbrella against the bleak December rain. Her feet were numb with cold. He had always pulled away from her when she'd climbed into bed with her feet like that. 'Warm those things before you put them on me.' She heard him saying it as she stood on the department store grating, the warm air billowing out her skirt.

He'd said it in Cabourg because each night, before she went to bed, she stood for a long time on the terrazzo in the bathroom combing out her hair. 'Come to bed,' he'd call out impatiently, 'You've been in there for hours.'

But she liked the smallness of that room, its safeness, the soothing routine of slowly untangling her hair. Leaving that room was leaving something safe. To go to the sea. To the edge. To the very rim of the world.

During the time she had known him, to her he personified the sea, sullen and unpredictable, and she was a traveller, a voyager drawn to water, an inexperienced sailor in danger of death.

Before she met him she had never even seen the sea and so, when she came to bed frightened and lay her naked body against his, she always felt that she was in danger of drowning.

Remembering that, Elkie closed her eyes. She wanted the sensation of darkness. She liked the dark. She felt safe—alone—in the dark.

She remembered the first night they spent together. When they were drunk, they danced in the dark. He promised to takc her one day to Paris and she, wanting to believe him, had believed him.

In Paris their room would overlook the Seine. In Paris she would wear open-toed shoes with glass fruit stitched to the toe and twist her long hair around chignons and make coin wishes in the fountains. In Paris they would make love in a cast-iron bed and listen to the bells of Notre Dame and see the canopies of the booksellers from their window and he would love her in the darkness on the bed near the Seine and they would have breakfast served on a silver tray and drink black coffee from small cups and when it rained they would hold each other on the iron bed in the darkness near the Seine and he would love her.

Double-eejit, she thought, how could you have been so bloody stupid. She composed her face as she walked towards the street vendor on the corner. She wasn't hungry, but she bought a bag of roasted chestnuts outside the department store where she worked, its famous animated windows dressed in a foot of artificial snow.

Near the main doors a busker sat on a stool playing an accordion. Hanging from the front of his instrument was a photograph of him as a young pugilist in baggy trunks, his boxer's nose broken even then. He sang, '"Christmas is coming, the geese are getting fat, won't you please put a penny in an old man's hat?"' Elkie saw the shoppers hurry past him in the rain. '"If you haven't got a penny, a halfpenny will do, if you haven't got a halfpenny, then God bless you."'

She threw some coins into his cap and thought of Mrs Ducker's bulldog face this morning at her door. 'And when will you have the rest of it then? Mr Ducker doesn't like to be kept waiting for his rent money. That's the trouble with young people today. They don't know the meaning of financial obligation—'

Elkie forced the landlady's strident voice to fade, to evaporate slowly into the crowd; it was like the annoying stink of a putrid cologne. Mrs Ducker would have her rent money; she'd just have to wait a little longer for it. She'd only found this job recently and, like most firms, they paid their wages a month in arrears.

As she hurried towards the underground, she ate the last of the chestnuts, mentally composing the letter she needed to write when she got home. It was another begging letter, but the begging didn't bother her any more, although at one time it had. She couldn't have cared less. She didn't care about anything any more. The last postcard she had received was from Lake Como: *After it rained all week we gave up and drove back towards Bergamo and thought we'd try again a few days later. The weather did improve on the second visit, though the light was not as good as it is meant to be on Lake Como. Every night we went to bed hoping for better weather, but it never happened.*

We; that pronoun had been burned into her memory. *We* must mean that he had another mistress, or that he was married and lived in a country house with wild foxes outside the door.

Mammy, she'd write, *sorry for being so long with this letter.* Even after five months, I still can't believe that he is gone. *You'll be glad to know* there's never going to be any wedding or nice weather or orange-blossom shoes. He left a 'prentice sailor; the weather got too rough. *I've finally found a job; I'm selling lingerie. At the interview I told them I hadn't any experience before* of being in love; I'd only read about it in books *and that I'd go overboard with enthusiasm because I wanted that job, was genuinely eager to learn. It's not a huge salary, but at least I can start to pay my own way. Could I borrow a fiver till payday? I'm a bit short again with the rent.*

She would tell her mother other things, too, in the letter, but she would not tell her why she was so eager to find a job in lingerie. It had to do with that *We* postcard, a presentiment that sooner or later he would walk into that fabulous store where she worked to buy something intimate for his new wife or mistress.

As Christmas neared her expectations grew stronger. They

came each night when the large, neon lights on the floor went out, one by one. It was her feeling that in the darkness she would see him, that she would see him in the crowds that hurried past her in the store, that he would suddenly appear walking towards her with his hands in his pockets, and he would see her standing behind her lingerie counter and there would be no more postcards for him to hide behind any more.

When she got home that night, Elkie dropped *Anna Karenina* on the hearth of the blocked-off fireplace. She lit its flimsy cover. The cardboard skirts of the dancers flared up brilliantly and then the flames died out.

'Damn you!' she said relighting it. The edges curled, but the dancers' faces were serene; the flames had gone out again. They were briefly safe from immolation.

Impatiently Elkie began ripping single pages out and wadding them into balls. She balanced the book on a pyre of paper and set it alight. She was watching the smoke with grim satisfaction when there was a knock at her door. 'Miss Bonner? Miss Bonner, are you all right? Are you in there?'

'Yes to both questions, Mrs Ducker.'

'Shall I call the Fire Brigade? I'm sure I smell smoke inside your room.'

'Everything's all right here, thank you very much.'

The landlady started to pound the door. 'Well if everything's all right in there, let me see for myself! What are you doing?'

'I'm burning a book.'

'Burning a book? You let me in or I'll let myself in! If you've set fire to my furniture, you'll pay for it!'

To her surprise, Elkie opened the door. It was so sudden that Mrs Ducker, from the force of her last blow, nearly fell into the room. 'What's going on here then?' she said, trying to regain her composure. 'What have you done?'

'Feel free to wander about my room. When you've seen for yourself that your precious furniture's intact, maybe you'll leave me alone.'

'What caused that smoke?'

'Can you not hear? I told you I was burning a book.'

'Why can't you throw it away? You aren't meant to burn books. In my house you aren't meant to burn anything.'

'Why don't you just get out of my room?' Elkie said.

'You haven't paid your rent, and you think that entitles you to burn the place down—'

'You old cow! You'll have your rent money soon enough. You've seen for yourself I'm not burning anything down. I'm burning something up. Now get out of my room. I'm not hurting your property, so it's none of your fucking business what I'm doing.'

'Well!' Mrs Ducker said, 'That's gratitude for you! I knew I should have turned you out on the street when that doctor came.'

'You shouldn't jump to conclusions, you old bag. I suffer from low blood pressure. I'm in the habit of fainting. It runs in the family. And now that I've treated you to my medical history, you can kindly get out of my room. If you don't, I'll call the police and tell them you're trespassing.'

'Well I never!' she said, backing towards the door. 'Well I never!'

Elkie slammed the door in her face. She could feel the vibrations in the floor, see them in the lone picture that hung on the plasterboard wall; fainter now she heard the sound of the landlady stomping down the uncarpeted stair.

She went to the hearth and picked up the book. The dead flames had singed Anna's yellow ball gown. She flipped through it, stopping at the page where Anna's brother asked Matvey if he thought a reconciliation was possible between himself and his wife. Elkie read aloud,

'Oblonsky was silent for a moment. Then a kind, rather pathetic smile appeared on his handsome face.

"Well? What do you think, Matvey?" he said, shaking his head.

"It's nothing, sir. Things will right themselves," replied Matvey.

"Right themselves?"

"That's it, sir." '

III THE END OF SUMMER, 1968

How I hug my antique grief to me,
it keeps me warm.

Victor Rowe, 'Night Time'

21

and leaving a trail across the puddles
of stops, hooks, tails,
like treble clefs they resound after
the departed train.
Natalya Gorbanyevskaya

There is a place where if we are wise it is thin, and if we are fools, it is thick. I think of love.

It's been a year today since you left me in Cabourg and I'm sad. I don't know why. There is no reason, rather there is cause for celebration. In three weeks, Ivan, I shall be a wife.

My fiancé kisses the nape of my neck. I shiver, never understanding why there, only there, it causes such tingling.

He offers me chocolate. How can I refuse? It's like refusing extreme unction. Chocolate. I cannot bear the taste. I take three squares.

'You can blame my aunt for my sweet tooth,' Michael is saying. 'After mummy died, she was always feeding me sweets.' A passion of his begun in childhood: brandy balls, Battenburg cake, liquorice lace, but chocolate especially. He hands me more chocolate, a niggertoe nut dipped in brown syrup. I hide it in a ball of dust that grows ever bigger beneath my bed.

As my fiancé, he wants to know the circumstances of my deflowering. As if it were of consquence now! Perhaps I should lie, embroider the unsavoury truth? No. He was a soldier and had not bothered to wash.

I've forgotten that soldier-boy, Ivan. I wonder, if things had been different, would I have forgotten you? Looking back on it, I'm trying to remember what I liked in you: your asking me to help you button your cuffs in the morning, touching your hand in the street. It was hard not to take it. We had to be discreet; people you knew might be watching. But I wanted them to see us together. You didn't. You were ashamed of me. You were afraid of what they might repeat.

After you left me, I went to bed with other men, lots of men. Perhaps you thought that if I loved you I wouldn't, but I couldn't wait forever. You see, I am dangerous, too.

The first lover I had after you'd gone thought he had successfully seduced me. I was lying naked on his bed and when he touched me, I began to cry. He was kind; he asked no questions; he just said, 'Get dressed and I'll take you home.'

The next morning I went out and bought new clothes and shoes and matching hose and a collapsible umbrella. I had my hair cut and I glued on false nails; I felt really glam. I kept walking in front of the lingerie mirror because I didn't recognize myself. Teetering on those black, spiked heels, the first pair I'd ever owned. I kept swanning in front of that mirror, laughing and crying at the same time, because I knew how ridiculous it all was: I'd go home to the same old room and to the same old snake that had managed to wriggle itself into a newer skin.

Mammy and my da begged me to come home but I wouldn't, not until I could walk down Main Street with my head held high. You see, they'd put an announcement in the paper about our engagement. The whole town thought that Elkie Bonner had been jilted. Jilted! The whole of Dungiven knew. There'd been some ugly rumours too, and I didn't feel the need to explain my running away to anyone.

And the postcards. I never understood why you bothered. They kept arriving. I keep the two Virgins above the bed, the ones you sent from Florence. They smile sweetly down on me and Michael. Only I know on the back is written: *Here are two of the nicest smiles I could find.*

The postcards kept arriving: Amsterdam and your initials, Zürich and your initials, Lake Como and your initials: *We went to bed hoping for better weather, but it never happened.*

How many months is it now? You never had any intention of writing even those postcards, but you couldn't help yourself, could you? That was to have been the end: the short, sweet goodbye in Cabourg, the chin-chin, and then those damn postcards kept dribbling in with no return address. I pinned them up around my four walls and took them all down again.

And even if I'd had your address, what would I have said? That potatoes cost two shillings a pound and that I'd lost a stone in weight and that mammy wrote saying my da had sold my old, green bicycle to the scrap man?

I keep thinking of that picture of you with Flash between your legs. You said that dog lived for the day you would come home, that after you went to boarding school in England the waiting kept him alive. That for years after you'd left home, that old dog would disappear for an hour every afternoon, and that your mother finally found out where he went to every day, down to the cemetery where you used to sit with him waiting at your father's grave.

I sit in my chair and burn candles, but you haven't written, not Sunday or Monday or the three months before that. Did you think that if I'd had your address, that I'd have run after you? Well, you're right there. I would have run to ultima Thule; I would have run to the rim of the world.

I used to sit and pray that you'd come. If I wore this and did that, you'd come. If I pinned up my hair in permanent-wave clips and put fresh garlic in my soup. I didn't know what to do. So I'd pick up your postcards and read them, over and over again: *We drove back towards Bergamo. The light was not as good as it is meant to be on Lake Como.*

So little light, Ivan, so little light in the world.

'The world's your oyster,' mammy used to say and, like a loon, I believed her. Just when you believe you have something that will last, the rug's taken from beneath your feet, and all you find you have is a window with a view you'd liked once, and now you can't remember why.

Pellipar, the avenue, the way it looked like Russia. I waited for you at the puddle where we'd met, hoping that you'd come. I watched my reflection in the water, and when it rained and my dress stuck to my legs and my hair made me look like a drowned rat, I half-hoped you wouldn't come just then and see me looking like that. That's what the world does to you. Mammy used to say that I wasn't ready for the world and I'd hate her for saying that, but I wasn't. Nobody is. Nobody.

It doesn't matter. The rain never stops. It keeps raining and raining. I never think about my other lovers. I don't even remember what that soldier-boy looked like. But your face, your face is tattooed on my skin.

I never told you mammy used to take off her flannel underwear and hide it in the bushes on the way to school, and then put it on again on the way back so the town girls wouldn't laugh at her. Or my da who, as a boy, played the tuba in a band. He bought an old tuba that most of the copperplating had worn off of; it was all he could afford. And before his first big parade, he'd sat and polished that tuba for hours and hours till it was as shiny as new, and then by the morning of the big parade, it had turned all green again.

I vowed at the beginning I'd never let you know me. There was too much I was ashamed of; there was too much I felt I had to hide.

I remember you said that your mother told you that one day you were going to get your comeuppance, and you said that you were still waiting. But you had such an easy life, Ivan. You never had to fight. You never had to dispose of a child before it was born. To make a decision and whatever you did was wrong, whichever choice you made. You said you were just waiting to die. I never told you I already had.

I'm changing the lock on my door. I didn't want to ask for my key back. I couldn't make myself do that. No. That isn't true; I'm lying. Mr Ducker is changing the lock because of a burglary. You never had a key. I often thought I'd offer you one. I never felt safe enough. I never felt safe.

You thought I belonged to you. I didn't. Do your lovers keep you awake? We never slept when we were together. You never understood it. I did. Knocking at my door at two in the morning. You said you'd always slept with other lovers. *I* knew why.

You wouldn't know me now. I'm reckless, carefree. But there was a time when I waited outside Helen Doran's, waited outside places we'd been together having this feeling, this presentiment, that you might be there. And every night I'd dream I saw you walking towards me with your hands in your pockets, and there'd be no place any more for you to hide.

The dream went on for a year and I had my lovers, one after another. I couldn't wait forever. Then I met Michael; the dream stopped. It was a relief of sorts. There is no relief.

You would hardly know me now. My breasts hang full like moons. My bottom teeth are crooked; my hair is turning grey. It's death I'm experiencing, prematurely like the hairs.

I lied to myself and said that it was best, that the last night in Cabourg you pretended nothing was different, and we made love, and then you left me the next morning never intending to come back. But I lay in that bed and thought, I see very clearly. I'm no coward. In the morning you will be gone.

Watching Michael pull off his boots, each evening a tug-o'-war. 'Give me a hand, Elkie,' he says, and puts the box of Black Magic on the bed. Grabbing a wet boot, pulling for all my worth. Never would buy a pair large enough to fit him. Says he likes tight boots because it makes him think. Many the time flying across the room with a boot in my hand. One of those men who can't make love unless his feet are bare.

I say I long for the warm bosom of Abraham. He doesn't know the metaphor. I tell him the story of old Grand-da Bonner whose wish it was when he died, for his family and friends to gather together and kill all his chickens. And while he was laid out, he wanted the birds to be fried up for a big chicken dinner, and for the biggest drumstick to be wedged between his dentures. He wanted to meet Abraham at the Pearly Gates with a mouthful of unchewed chicken. The death I speak of is purely a state of mind.

He asks again about my 'deflowering'. Sounds gentle. Wonder why they call it that? Like I say, I've forgotten his face, the one who came courting and then, after a few visits, pulled me into my da's shed and threw my skirts in the air. I bit my lip, seeing the white skirt flying, the slip billowing down. Wincing at the inflated size of it, virgin-tight.

We had been drinking and, even so, the pain was terrible. I had only managed a carrot before, with some difficulty. At nineteen I was beginning to despair of never being pierced, but he did it for me gladly, a soldier-boy just back from the Mediterranean. He wooed me with a bottle of Marsala.

He hadn't even bothered to wash. He said soldiers were forced to practise self-pleasure, as though it was something they had to do on the shooting range. But I wasn't concerned about that; I was more concerned 'with child, with young, big with, consequences, etc.' Hating him, I couldn't wait for him to dismount. He asked, 'Was I too big for ye?' and I was crying to beat the band so I nodded, so I wouldn't have to answer, so I wouldn't have to explain myself. It was innocence that was gone.

Those vain and preening lovers! I listed them by initial on my calendar, never giving their names or what dull things they said, only their initial and the night they inserted themselves: P. who gave me bruises, purple welts on my buttocks. He pinched and kissed passionately though he tended to slobber. E. who'd studied philosophy and had come to the dry conclusion that what was termed love was only impractical desire. C. who travelled for a living, spending mere hours with me en route, agitated if I should be suffering from the curse. He got up each morning and thanked God for his prick-stick. I had no such affliction. I never knew his real name; I called him Caligula. He was better nameless, without a fixed address.

Where does all this end? Not with the spunk on the sheet or the blood on the mattress. O no. Shall I say no more, goodbye?

Watch your final, spectral retreat, leaving me to forget the tales of your family history: your aged mother, thick books on her lap about trollops and whores, the customs of suttee and purdah, the cities of Sodom and Gomorrah, the lands of Goshen and Hell. According to you, she never hung washing in the same room as herself because of 'miasmas' though when you asked, she never would say what they were, or why they were to be feared.

You said she never spilled salt without tossing it over both shoulders as she could never remember which. And black cats. It was bad luck only from one direction and she couldn't remember that either, and so was spooked, east or west, for days afterwards.

When a boy your misdemeanour offence: during the hours of darkness caused to be on a road on a vehicle, namely a bicycle, which did not carry a lamp showing to the front a white light and a lamp showing to the rear a red light at a visible distance.

I burned everything you gave me except the elephants. They live on the sill, two north, two south, on the ivory window-ledge. The biggest I call Malverna.

I've consigned you to hell. But you said there is no hell. You don't believe in the Fallen Angel, so you can't be incinerated. You said the only thing to truly fear is twice-used toilet paper.

Surely you have another lover by now. I try to imagine what she looks like, how you behave towards her, sitting in your garden until midnight. And I can see nothing: no face, no house, no garden. Just you, Ivan, staring at the world with your sad, sad eyes.

There's always travel. I could go on a world cruise. Pity I'd only meet widows in fire opals and seamed hose vomiting over the railings. I should have been a sailor given as I am to water, a voyager drawn to desert seas.

But there remains the question, where does all this end? Shall I drift from one infidel to the next, wary of pubic lice, pulling nits between thumb and forefinger and crushing them on white paper?

Flash died before seeing you again.

I remember when I asked you out of nervousness if you had ever loved anyone and you had answered, 'Yes.' That you'd wake up and touch the bed and then you'd jump up and search the rooms, and then you'd realize that she'd never been there at all. I wanted to ask who it was that you loved, but I didn't want to know. I didn't want to know what it was that had killed you, that had made you go dead inside.

I often wonder what kind of life you're leading. I try to imagine you with someone else. It's black. But I hope that you are happy, that you have found some happiness. You seemed so restless in spite of your wealth. You seemed to be looking for something, but you didn't know what it was. Do you remember the clowns? The wooden ones in Cabourg that jerked from side to side with their mouths open? It was as though they were in pain; it was as though they were screaming. I've often thought we were like those clowns.

Last night Michael and I went out and drank wine in a room with potted palms. Only a week now to the wedding. He sweated beside me; his forehead red and shiny. He loosened his tie on the veranda; he loosened the grip on my arm.

Afterwards he limped to a taxi; he was breaking in new boots. In the cab I cried. I stared at the glass canopies outside the white Georgian buildings. Nothing felt right; nothing felt safe.

Despite the heat he pulled me towards him and pressed me against his sweating body. He said, 'You depend on me too much.' And I answered, 'If I can't depend on you, Michael, who can I depend on?'

'Come on, Elkie,' he said. 'Smile. You never smile any more.' And then he made the cabbie stop in front of a candy shop, the window full of dark, handmade chocolates. In the middle of the display, in a heart-shaped arrangement, was a sign, PARMA VIOLET CREAMS.

He came out with a box of chocolates. He opened the lid, a tiny purple flower on top of each one. 'Have one,' he said, 'it'll cheer you up.' And I thought about funeral violets and extreme unction and the mints in the pockets of your smoking jacket and the melting niggertoes in the dust beneath my bed.

Inside the flat I powder his buttocks; I pull his cheeks apart. We make love and afterwards, emptiness. Emptiness. And I had wanted to fill his bowels with fire, to set ourselves alight.

We'll grow old together. I won't always look as I look now, able to bare my neck and throat. My breasts shrunken paps, his ballocks bulging, a touch of prostate. I say amen to all that, but now the cunt is filled and emptied and filled again, legs in the air quicker than one, two, three. I am never much good in accounting for it until we lie panting in the dark, like dogs.

I don't love him. I've never loved anyone except you.

I thought that if I married him, I'd change; I'd have to change, that the past would go away of its own accord. He asked me to marry him and I said, 'Yes.' Yes. Why not? Michael's nice enough. Safe enough. Too safe.

He touches me gently on the shoulder and asks, 'Why are you crying, Elkie?'

And I can't tell him it's because I'm cold and that nothing can warm me, that there's no going back. He has thin lips, just like you. I read a poem once about men with thin lips. The book fell open at that page. I wonder what might have happened if I'd been free when I met him, if there'd been no one else to think about. At what bridge would I be standing on now, Ivan, looking backwards?

But all I can see now is his small mouth and perfect, white teeth. 'Why are you crying?' he says. 'You're supposed to be happy. You're going to marry me in seven days,' and I answer, 'Yes, Michael, yes,' but all I can see is that poem, 'Beware the man whose mouth is small/For he'll give nothing and take all.' Michael's mouth eating Parma violet creams.

I still have the blue card from the dance on the river, your name on every line except the last.

Don't you see, Ivan, all I ever wanted was the last dance. I'll be your cotillion girl, a carnation behind my ear, one last spin around the floor before the lights . . . before the lights go out.

But it's already dark. There is no going back. There's a wife now, a garden, a house in the country with foxes outside the door, a river.

You're the cold, deep river that runs down the middle of me, the hungry river that each night swallows the moon.

IV FALL, 1980

You refuse to give up.
You go on hoping.
You collect the fingerprints
of every catastrophe,
hoping to catch them red-handed.
The snow falls doubly.
Suddenly we have grey hair,
both of us.

Antonín Bartušek, 'Those few years'

22

It was on such a day . . . that I found myself,
all my senses wide open, on one of Fialta's steep
little streets, taking in everything at once,
that marine rococo on the stand, and the coral
crucifixes in a shop window, and the dejected
poster of a visiting circus, one corner of its
drenched paper detached from the wall.

Vladimir Nabokov, 'Spring in Fialta'

He'd driven too fast since Paris, often in the chicken lane on the three-lane highway, exhilarated at his own foolishness. He'd had to leave Orly later than he'd planned; the flight from Zürich had been delayed. He was making up for lost time. Lost time had obsessed him lately. In a few days he'd be forty-nine.

Outside Etretat he got out of the car to stretch his legs. He walked to the edge of a cliff. They'd had a picnic there, just over the edge. He had swum in the sea; she had waded, collected a skirtful of shells. He had taken her to Etretat to show her the cliffs, the three, limestone legs carved out of the rock by peasants who would soon revolt, to show her what starving men had been forced to do to provide Marie Antoinette with her choicest beds of oysters.

She had worn the hat that day, had insisted on wearing it. He could still see her sitting there in its narrow shade, the huge flowers around the crown. Where they'd had their picnic, two skiffs lay like dead minnows, belly-side up on the sand.

He wouldn't climb down now. She might have arrived by now. He smiled to himself as he hurried back to the Peugeot parked above the tall, dead grass.

It was past the height of the tourist season. The hotels in the resort town were almost empty. The iron tables of the sidewalk cafés, once cluttered with glasses and dishes and the elbows of lovers, were bare.

At the sea-end of the Avenue de la Mer, paint blistered on the façade of the Grand Hotel. The summer awnings over the dining-room windows had been removed. The carefully tended boxes of flowers beneath them were dying.

Twenty kilometres from Proust's Balbec Hotel, a convoy carrying animals and machinery moved slowly down the flat, coast road. On the panels of the trucks were painted fierce tigers.

The lorries' headlights, bright as cats' eyes, winked at the winding asphalt, the marshland to the south, and to the dark sleeve of the sea. When they reached Cabourg, the lorries drove off the road and formed a circle in a grassy field. The drivers climbed out of their cabs and yawned. The enamelled cats snarled into the cool September night.

At eight that evening she registered at the Hotel Fatima on the Avenue Pasteur. The hotelier insisted on her passport and the night's payment in advance. He counted the money she gave him, then pushed the key brusquely towards her across the high desk. He motioned towards the first floor with a mutilated thumb.

Chambre 103: the room's bare electric bulb illuminated two startled cockroaches, a small table, a sagging double bed, a bidet and a huge wardrobe with a full-length mirror that stood sentry near the door.

She picked up the heavy, glass ashtray on the table. On the bottom was painted *Bienvenu à Cabourg*. 'Welcome to Cabourg,' she repeated, and started to laugh. It was the only object in the room that had any pretensions of welcome.

Elkie threw her suitcase on the bed. The one dress she had folded so carefully was crushed. The georgette dress had creased in the small suitcase even though she had protected it with tissue paper and had packed it on top.

Unpacking, she thought about the card that had taken her to this room, the postcard he had sent requesting their meeting. On the front a Bonnard nude, on the back a short message: *Will be at the resort the last week in September. Want to see you.*

It had stunned her. She had put it on the mantelpiece in her room almost afraid to handle it, a postal wafer that might melt with the touch of her hand. Feeling frightened she'd thrown it away and then had retrieved it. Twice. With the coach ticket in her bag she'd gone on a last-minute shopping spree and had bought all the wrong things: a sleeveless cocktail dress, a boa stole, a half-price tube of suntan cream.

She dressed by candlelight and stood in front of the mirror in her gown and feathered stole. A draught of wind blew the flame aslant and her elongated shadow danced on the fenestrated wall.

She stared at herself critically in the soft light and wondered what to do when she saw him. What would she say; what was there to say: How are you, Ivan? Can it really have been thirteen years? I've been frozen for so long.

Elkie woke with the light on her face; in her excitement last night she had forgotten to close the curtains. She reached under her pillow for the postcard and re-read it for the hundredth time. Ever since she'd received it two weeks ago she'd been agitated, slightly breathless.

She went into the bathroom and turned the hot water tap on full. Her one extravagance, a room with its own bath. She looked into the water at her slightly magnified body, her rippling reflection, the water's shining surface another kind of mirror.

She closed her eyes and tried to remember some of the town's landmarks: the place where old men had played their never-ending games of *boules,* that bronze statue in a memorial garden. But try as she might, she could not remember what the subject was: a moustachio'd French general or a moustachio'd French general on a horse? And she laughed, realizing that it didn't matter. That nothing mattered except the fact that she was here.

She talked to herself; for the moment there was no one else to talk to, thinking out loud that she must look up the phrase for, Can I leave these in your safe? The four, teak elephants she wanted to lock away were quite worthless, but of great sentimental value.

She held her breath and slid beneath the water. She knew that in third-class hotels you could never tell what the chambermaids might think worth stealing.

She headed in the direction of the sea. Along the Avenue de la Mer she saw posters announcing the arrival of a circus. Posters with tawdry illustrations of lion tamers and tigers, colourful rectangles pasted to the wall of a derelict store.

As she neared the promenade she was disappointed to see that the hub of the resort had a look of decayed elegance, of a seaside-bathing town that had perhaps outlived its time. She saw a provincial place, a backwater. Perhaps it had been like that before and she had failed to notice it, but the Grand Hotel, she thought, surely the hotel had been whiter than that.

She circled it, feeling as though she had been let out of prison. The vague familiarity of it all: the steep Norman roofs, the wet, iron tables, the shop fronts, the deserted promenade, amazed that these things could evoke a feeling she had long denied herself, to which she had become a stranger.

She stopped in a souvenir shop near the casino. It was filled with racks of dusty postcards, glittered seashells, pink rock moulded in the form of a woman's leg. Because she found them so ugly she bought half a dozen, a chorus line of half-bent cancan legs.

With them dancing in a paper bag, she wandered down the promenade. His card had been so imprecise. As she walked in the direction of the hat shop, she remembered their first night: the way they had danced, like Anna and Vronsky, how she kept falling off her shoes. After all these years he wanted to see her again and she did not know why. Perhaps he did not know himself.

The day stretched out before her like the sea, cold and grey, and she could not imagine the end of it.

Ivan passed the casino to the left of the Grand Hotel. Leaves and paper wrappers had collected in the unswept threshold of the double doors. A faded sign said, The Grand Hotel Casino Will Be Closed Until April. He shielded his eyes as he stared into the darkened passageway crowded with up-ended chairs.

'Monsieur, monsieur!' a voice called out behind him.

He turned around; it was Jean, the head croupier of the casino. He was wearing his light cotton uniform even though the season had ended. '*Bonjour*,' the old man said extending his hand. 'Long time no see, as you English say. *Ça va bien?*'

'I'm fine, Jean. And you?' He could not help noticing the redness of the croupier's face, the slight palsy of his free hand.

'I am fine too. It's good to see you again. Why have you come so late this year?'

'Business,' he lied. 'I couldn't get away any earlier. I was just going to the hotel for a drink. Would you like to join me?'

Ivan chose an umbrellaed table on the terrace of the Grand Hotel. They seated themselves in damp, iron chairs.

The waiter brought their drinks; Ivan raised his glass. '*A votre santé.*'

'*A votre santé.*'

'And you,' Ivan said, looking anxiously down the mile-long promenade, 'why are you still here? I'd have thought you wanted to get away from this place.'

'Me?' The croupier shook his head. 'No. I'm sad when the season ends. To the others it's only a job. The flower sellers, the girls who sell Italian ices. They leave as soon as they can. I hate it when it's like this. When it's dead. And here you are,' he said, 'you who should know better, coming at this time of year.'

'I don't like crowds anymore. I must be getting old. I like to have the town to myself.'

'You like to have it to yourself,' the old man said. 'I see.' They were silent for a moment, each lost in their own thoughts.

The wind snapped the slack cloth between the ribs of the

umbrellas as though it was uneasy of their silence, as though it had to provide the conversation they could not find.

After a while Jean looked up and said, 'How long will you be staying?'

'I'm not sure. It depends.'

He tipped his glass back. 'Perhaps I'll see you before you go.' As he pushed himself up from his chair his head grazed a rib of the umbrella. '*Merde!*' he said, then laughed in embarrassment. 'I must tell Michel to put these away or they'll be useless in the spring. Thank you again for the drink.'

Jean turned back once and waved. He had heard the others gossip about him, that after the season ended their head croupier became a lush. No lights, no noise, like he'd said; he could not face the silence of being alone. Jean is an old man, they'd said, Jean has never had anything but his work, and it won't be long until he doesn't even have that.

As Ivan watched him walk unsteadily down the promenade his mother's funeral came back to him, the words she'd chosen to have carved on her headstone: 'And the floors shall be full of wheat and the vats shall overflow with wine and oil. And I will restore to you the years that the locust hath eaten.' He remained seated on the terrace and felt cold. He knew the sea breeze had nothing to do with it.

23

Thumb-filling his pipe from a rubber pouch as he walked, a plus-foured Englishman of the solid exportable sort came from under an arch and entered a pharmacy, where large pale sponges in a blue vase were dying a thirsty death behind their glass.

Vladimir Nabokov, 'Spring in Fialta'

The shops along the seafront hadn't changed much. I went into the hat shop and asked after the woman who'd sold me the straw hat. They told me she had died.

The window was filled with wooden stands and large, felt hats with feathers. I asked to see some of them. A shop assistant unlocked the display case. I took out one of the largest hats and stood in front of a mirror that had been placed in the middle of the counter. I said, 'These hats look a bit old-fashioned.'

The young salesgirl clucked her tongue. 'They're the old girl's hats. Some of the last she made. She wouldn't follow the fashion. She kept making hats like that—' She blushed when she realized that she'd pointed to the hat I had on. 'She kept making hats with wide brims when no one wanted them. The shop was empty all the time. One morning she didn't come in to work. They found her in her kitchen. She'd gassed herself.'

I glimpsed my face in the mirror. My mouth had dropped open. The hat flopped over my right eye. I turned from side to side slowly, took it off, and put it on the counter. 'I'll take it,' I said.

The shop girl stared at me in disbelief, then went into the back room for a box. It wasn't large enough and she disappeared behind the curtains again. She returned, put the hat in the box and buried it in tissue paper. She secured it with string and made a loop on top for my finger.

I paid a ridiculously high price for it. I knew I wouldn't wear it more than once. It didn't matter. I watched my reflection in the yellow cellophane which kept the hats in the window from fading. There was a card in one corner they'd forgotten to remove,

Mme F. Deshouillers, Modiste
Chapeaux pour Jour et Soir
351, Promenade Marcel Proust
High School English Spoken Here

I walked down the promenade, the huge box banging against my leg. There weren't many people out. A stone staircase led to the beach. Rounded brown stones had been washed ashore and were lying on the wet sand. They reminded me of turtle eggs. I stood on them as I took off my shoes, then put them with the hatbox.

From where I stood I could see where the beach curved like a small arm. I could also see the stone steps there that went into the sea. That last afternoon we'd sat on those steps. He took off his shoes and hung his feet in the water.

I was still smarting from the argument we'd had at breakfast. We'd eaten outside the hotel. I'd kicked the bottom of the table because I knew it would embarrass him. He shouted at me about my behaviour until he saw a waiter approach our table. The waiter asked if anything was wrong.

Ivan said, 'Everything is fine. Fine.' I turned away from the table and stared at the gravel drive. The waiter made some pretence of staying near us and we couldn't continue our argument. After breakfast we sulked and walked in silence to the beach.

While he paddled his feet in the cold water, he was planning his escape. He moved one step down, then another and another, until the water covered his knees. I thought he might swim away. Instead he asked if I wanted a cream cake. He looked up at me and asked, 'What are you laughing at?'

'Nothing,' I said. 'I didn't laugh.'

'But I heard you.'

'You're mistaken.'

I didn't even realize I'd laughed. I laughed so little then that the sound was strange to me, as though it belonged to someone else.

We didn't go straight to the patisserie but walked through a field. The grass was lush in places and baked yellow and flat in others. There was a row of willows at one end of the field. We walked in that direction, further and further apart, like two planets losing their gravitational force.

Ivan said, 'I have to leave tomorrow. I must take care of some financial matters.'

'You've never mentioned it before!' I said.

'It hasn't been important before. I know it's sooner than you expected, but there are certain things I'm responsible for.'

'Yes,' I said, 'I'm sure there are.'

'You can stay on in the hotel.'

'I'll go home and save you some money.'

'Look, I promised you a holiday. Just because I'm going doesn't mean you have to cut yours short.'

I screamed, 'Jesus, do you think I want to wander around the town on my own?'

'There was never anything between us,' he said. 'Surely you must have known that.' Afterwards, I was never sure if he'd said those words, or if I'd only imagined them. I was so stunned that I stumbled and fell. He brushed the grass off my dress and handed me my shoe. 'We shouldn't have come this way,' he said.

I remember the cake I ate after that. It was a square, iced in chocolate and filled with cream. It was sprinkled with tiny, chocolate shavings.

'This is one of my favourite places,' he said. 'I come here every year.'

I didn't know if it was France or the patisserie he was talking about, but it didn't matter. I was concentrating on keeping the fixed expression on my face. I was numb, because if I allowed myself to feel anything, even the china cup burning my fingers, I was lost.

'My father discovered Cabourg when he drove back from Bayeux once.'

'How interesting,' I said, forcing the last of the cake into my mouth. He looked at me as though I were mad.

'It's too busy now. It was a mistake to come at this time of year. How do you like your cake?'

'It's brilliant,' I said. 'I think I'll have another.'

I ate six cream cakes that day. It was a record. I didn't even like the bloody cakes after the first one, but he was going in the morning on the eight o'clock train, and I wanted him sitting in the chair opposite me so that I could memorize his face . . .

Poor Ivan! Me trying to make him into Vronsky, into the storybook character he never was. You just didn't know what to make of me, wild as an Indian, when all you were used to were rich, society girls. I'll bet none of them filled up notebook after notebook about you, writing love letters they never had the courage to send. But I'll bet you never sent any of them postcards. They wouldn't have lived with them like I did. Lived with them like lovers—dangerous, illicit, hidden beneath the bed.

Tuesday, my second day, and no sign of him yet. It would be pointless asking to see the registration book at the Grand Hotel. He never used his real name when he came here. I don't remember the other name after all these years.

I packed one dress he had seen me in; I'm wearing it. If he doesn't recognize me, he might recognize the dress. But it's very thin and wrinkled, and not really warm enough to wear.

I bought it for the first time I came here. The new straw hat matched it perfectly. The woman who gassed herself said, 'I have just the hat for that dress!' She reached into the window and brought out the hat sitting on the tips of her fingers. It was unbleached straw, the crown circled with red flowers. She led me to a mirror on the counter and sat me on a stool. She pressed my hair down and put the hat on. She held a hand mirror so that I could see the back of it and said, 'You look like such a lady in that hat!'

I did feel like a lady. The hat was more than I could afford, but I thought that Ivan would be pleased. I'll never understand why he threw it into the sea. He didn't know what that hat meant to me, or what it cost. He never knew the true cost of anything.

I think I'll have a drink in that bar. A nice nut brandy. That's what we used to drink. They served it in glasses shaped like Easter lilies. It was sweet and hot going down.

He told me I was drinking too much. He didn't know why. So I won't feel, Ivan. So I won't feel so much. But I never said that. He would never have understood that. All he ever understood were foreign languages, and what knife and fork to use at dinner.

I'll take a walk past the hotel again. Nothing much has changed. It's a bit shabbier, needs a few coats of fresh paint.

I told him the Grand Hotel revolving door was the first one I'd ever seen. 'Kiss me,' I said while we were in that door.

'Silly girl, you aren't supposed to get in the same compartment as me.'

'Kiss me,' I said.

'In the room,' he said. He looked so embarrassed when we stumbled into the foyer coming out of the same compartment.

I wonder why I bothered to come back. The postcard only said, *Will be at the resort the last week of September. Want to see you.* No return address. There never was on any of the cards he'd sent these last thirteen years. Just a scribbled message usually about the weather: *Sitting in Amsterdam in sunshine. First time it has stopped raining.*

Every year a few postcards from different places. I've got them all tied up with string. It didn't take his postcards to make me remember him. I only had to look at my face; it was written all over my face.

I did try to forget. I was even engaged once. Michael gave me a little opal ring when he proposed. I told him opals were unlucky and he said, 'Don't be silly. That's superstitious nonsense.'

I knew opals were unlucky, and sure enough, from the minute he gave me the ring, things began to go sour. He kept pressing me for a date for the wedding, and I kept postponing it. And what's worse, I hated his damp house and the spinster aunt he lived with.

One Sunday when he'd gone out for some chocolates, his aunt said there were a few questions she wanted to ask me because Michael's parents were dead and she was the only one to act in his better interests. 'But before we discuss that,' she said, 'I want you to know that as you and Michael can't afford a home of your own, you're more than welcome to live here with me.'

I couldn't think of anything worse. I knew she hated me and was only asking because she'd raised Michael and couldn't bear the thought that he would leave her. 'Now,' she said, 'do you think you're really ready for marriage?'

I started to laugh. I was less controlled in those days than I am now. She didn't know anything about marriage. She'd never had anything between her legs except a bicycle. I looked her straight in the eye and said, 'Is anyone really ready for anything?'

She told me that I shouldn't be flippant, that she'd asked me a serious question and she expected a serious answer. She said that men were different from women; they were just like animals. She said it was her duty to tell me that Michael wasn't pure, that he'd known women, had known them in the biblical sense. I told her I wasn't entirely innocent of other men myself and to keep her bloody nose out of what didn't concern her.

'How dare you speak to me like that!' she said. 'You're nothing but trash. My nephew marrying trash!'

'I wouldn't worry your head then,' I told her, 'because I'm not marrying him.' I dropped the opal ring in the plate of Battenburg cake and walked out.

That was where the engagement ended, in that museum of a house in Willesden with its snowfall of lace doilies. I knew I'd done the right thing. Her precious nephew would have suffocated me.

And every morning after that, I was all right until I realized that I was alone. After you're alone for so long, you know you'll always be alone. It's taken all these years to learn to accept it, and then, then this bloody card comes. My world turned upside down. I thought, I can't go; there's no point in going. He might not be there; it might be a hoax. And here I am, standing in front of this damn hotel in a thirteen-year-old dress! Well, like they say, there's no fool like an old fool.

I'll sit on the Avenue de la Mer and watch the world go by. Even if he isn't here, if I don't see him, it doesn't matter. Not really. I've learned to live by myself. Nobody can take that away from me. I wonder if he's got all his hair. But it doesn't matter. Nothing matters, just to sit here drinking black coffee and watching the world go by.

I shouldn't have worn this dress. Georgette is much too thin for this time of year. Much too thin. I'll catch my death of cold sitting here in the wind. I must go to my room and get my coat. It's madness to sit here in this dress.

People are staring at me. Maybe it's the hat. I'll order another coffee. I don't give a damn what they think. I can sit here as long as I like. I can look for him with this hat on. I can see out from under the brim and no one watching me will know I'm looking for someone I know. People get the wrong impression when they see a woman sitting alone.

I can see who goes in and out of the hotel from here. Ivan might just go by. I hope I recognize him. I'm sure I will. He can't have changed that much.

There's someone who looks like him. Jesus, I wish I had my glasses with me. I hope I don't do anything silly when I see him, like cry. Jesus, I hope I don't cry. Anything but cry: laugh, fall off my shoes. Not cry. What the hell am I crying for? I finished crying years ago.

The waiter's staring at me. Or my hat or because I'm crying. No, it's no use sitting here. He's not coming. It's a joke. Someone's playing a joke on me, a cruel joke. Anyone could have sent that card, copied his writing: *Will be at the resort the last week of September* . . . Anyone could have copied it.

I can't stay here. I can't be away too long. I'll lose my job. Losing a job because I sat around in Cabourg for someone who's not going to come. I'm mad. I'll pack tonight. But it's only Tuesday. I'll stay one more day. I'll wear the dress just once more and if I don't see him, I'll go home—

24

Rummaging in your black memory you find
gloves up to the elbow,
and the Petersburg night.
Anna Akhmatova, 'Three Verses'

That evening he sat on the terrace of the Grand Hotel, the one that faced the sea. Around the fenced-off area small, white lights were strung in arcs. They were lit, faintly illuminating the half-dozen tables, the mist-covered chairs, the floral border of dying geraniums.

He slumped over the table; the swim he'd had earlier had exhausted him. Until four he had stayed close to the hotel, thinking that he was certain to see her. He was beginning to regret his card hadn't been more specific.

To pass the time he had leafed through a damp newspaper someone had left on the seat. Each time he flicked through it he saw a small article that disturbed him. 'The police,' it said, 'were trying to identify a woman killed as she walked in front of a lorry a mile west of Villerville. Her body was mutilated and there was no means of identification in her clothing. She was in her thirties and was wearing a black dress.'

He decided he was being silly. It couldn't be her. He'd just grown tired of waiting, of looking up and down the esplanade with no one but himself to talk to. He'd slept badly the past two nights; he decided to go for a cold swim.

He let the waves carry him out further than he'd ever been before. He couldn't feel his hands or feet as they cut through the water. As he swam he thought of her, he had thought of little else for days, how all the women he'd known were so unlike her, how collectively they'd left no impression. He had always cared for her with a fierceness he had not understood otherwise he would never have bothered to send her those absurd cards about the weather.

He dived into the waves, again and again, until he was exhausted, but it wasn't until he'd waded ashore that he realized he'd given up all hope of seeing her or he'd never have left his seaside table.

It was dusk when he heard the sound of a woman's shoes clipping on the promenade. As she passed him in the fading light he saw that she had red hair.

'*Fous le camp!*' she spat at him, '*Allez-vous-en!*'

'Oh,' he said, releasing her arm reluctantly, unable for a moment to hide his disappointment. 'Sorry. Sorry, I thought you were someone else.'

The woman smiled in embarrassment realizing that he was drunk, that he meant no harm. She started to walk away.

'Wait,' he said, 'won't you stay and have a drink?' He gestured towards his empty table, the candle flickering in its amber glass. If she drank with him she'd kill another hour before he went up to his room, but the woman just smiled at him as though he were mad and turned away.

He staggered back to the table. Stupid bitch, he thought, the stupid bitch didn't understand. He fell into his chair, almost knocking over a box of geraniums. He glanced down the promenade at her receding figure and slammed his fist down on the table.

The candlelight exaggerated his wrinkles, emphasized his baldness, the puffiness of his eyes. *And when she was bad, she was horrid*; the nursery rhyme kept going through his mind. Yes, her father had said at his mother's funeral last month, she's still at Mrs Ducker's, that wee flat she's always had on the third floor.

And he had never told her he loved her. From where he sat he could see the faint lights of the visiting circus, hear the faint sounds of the band.

CIRCUS PEOPLE written on her palm. She said she'd go down to the fairground to watch them. She liked the trapeze artists the best, flying through the air in those skintight suits. And when she'd asked him that night if he had ever loved anyone, he had said yes. He said he'd sleepwalk, sit bolt upright in the middle of the night, and begin to search the house. He'd call her name, call and call, and wake up, shivering. But when he had told that story, he had not named her. That she was the one he had loved, that she was the one he had shouted for, naked, in the night.

She walked to the train station, the last place she had seen him. It had been warm the morning he left. They sat on that bench near the double doors. He took a flower from the inside of his jacket. She had been all right until then, until she saw it: a pink carnation wilted from the heat. He gave it to her and said, 'I'm sorry it couldn't have been different,' and then the train pulled into the station, and he took his bags and climbed up the steps to the carriage door.

The windows of the train were down. He stood at one of them and waved. 'I'll write,' he said as the train was pulling out, and as the train gathered speed, she found herself running beneath his window. She ran the length of the platform, and then the platform ended and the train was gone.

Somehow she'd got home; she could hardly remember the journey. She'd stayed drunk for three days. She had recovered, but she'd never recovered. If she'd recovered, she'd be married to someone like Michael now and eating at home instead of sitting in cafés by herself, hiding under a hat so people wouldn't feel sorry for her. She didn't feel sorry for herself; she only felt foolish.

She walked back from the station, her arms crossed across her chest. The breeze lifted a portion of the large brim. It revealed only a triangle of her face.

She went over to the railing and leaned against it. There were only two boats out. She stood and watched them for a long time; in the morning she would be gone.

She wrapped her arms tighter around herself and continued walking towards her hotel which was at the opposite end of the beach. A hundred yards away was the Grand Hotel and she looked up briefly towards its upper floors.

When she looked down again, she saw a man standing at the railing looking out to sea. He was smoking a cigar; the wind carried his smoke towards her.

'Montecristos! I know that smell, I'd know it anywhere!' She walked towards him, her backless pumps making dull clips on the promenade. 'You'd think he'd turn around! He hears me coming. He knew I'd come. There was never any question I wouldn't. I never moved in case he wanted to reach me. No return address, I couldn't even write to him. Why won't he turn around?'

She started to call out his name and suddenly became afraid; she saw her shadow on the board walk. 'The hat!' Elkie reached up and touched the floppy brim. 'I've got the bloody hat on! My God, I look ridiculous! The first time in thirteen years wearing a thirteen-year-old dress! What will he think? That he made the right decision years ago, that's what he'll think!'

As she walked towards him she kept stumbling on the battens of the promenade. Why am I crying? she thought, I finished crying years ago.

'Ivan!' she called out. The man continued to stare straight ahead at the sea. '*Ivan*!' she called again, but it was not him. Even without her glasses she knew it was not him. She'd have to go back to the hotel and pack. The coach left for Paris at six in the morning. There was nothing to do now but go home. He hadn't come. Someone had played a joke on her but even if they hadn't, it was already too late. She knew that; she knew there were no second chances anyway.

She started towards the Hotel Fatima. As she walked past the Grand Hotel she didn't even see the man asleep at the table, the candlelight flickering on his bald head.

She looked back once, just once, and the man was still standing there facing out to sea and the white terrace lights were swinging.